HE TURNED TO KITTY

His hazel eyes twinkled for he could see that she did not wish to give him her hand. However, as Kitty stepped down, the hem of her skirt caught on the coach door hinge. She felt the tug on her skirt, looked round, lost her balance and went tripping forward. The earl caught her deftly in his arms, and for a long moment held her firmly. Blue eyes looked up and found hazel eyes alight with mischievous amber lights. Kitty was conscious of a new most foreign tingle of excitement. She found herself blushing as she breathed, "Thank you. I only hope I haven't torn my gown."

"Don't move," he answered as he reached round and bent to release her skirt from the doorway. "There. I don't believe it has been damaged." The earl's voice was soft and almost mesmerizing. Kitty felt as though she couldn't breathe. What was this?

ZEBRA'S REGENCY ROMANCES
DAZZLE AND DELIGHT

A BEGUILING INTRIGUE   (4441, $3.99)
by Olivia Sumner

Pretty as a picture Justine Riggs cared nothing for propriety. She dressed as a boy, sat on her horse like a jockey, and pondered the stars like a scientist. But when she tried to best the handsome Quenton Fletcher, Marquess of Devon, by proving that she was the better equestrian, he would try to prove Justine's antics were pure folly. The game he had in mind was seduction — never imagining that he might lose his heart in the process!

AN INCONVENIENT ENGAGEMENT   (4442, $3.99)
by Joy Reed

Rebecca Wentworth was furious when she saw her betrothed waltzing with another. So she decides to make him jealous by flirting with the handsomest man at the ball, John Collinwood, Earl of Stanford. The "wicked" nobleman knew exactly what the enticing miss was up to — and he was only too happy to play along. But as Rebecca gazed into his magnificent eyes, her errant fiancé was soon utterly forgotten!

SCANDAL'S LADY   (4472, $3.99)
by Mary Kingsley

Cassandra was shocked to learn that the new Earl of Lynton was her childhood friend, Nicholas St. John. After years at sea and mixed feelings Nicholas had come home to take the family title. And although Cassandra knew her place as a governess, she could not help the thrill that went through her each time he was near. Nicholas was pleased to find that his old friend Cassandra was his new next door neighbor, but after being near her, he wondered if mere friendship would be enough . . .

HIS LORDSHIP'S REWARD   (4473, $3.99)
by Carola Dunn

As the daughter of a seasoned soldier, Fanny Ingram was accustomed to the vagaries of military life and cared not a whit about matters of rank and social standing. So she certainly never foresaw her *tendre* for handsome Viscount Roworth of Kent with whom she was forced to share lodgings, while he carried out his clandestine activities on behalf of the British Army. And though good sense told Roworth to keep his distance, he couldn't stop from taking Fanny in his arms for a kiss that made all hearts equal!

Courting Christina

Claudette Williams

ZEBRA BOOKS
KENSINGTON PUBLISHING CORP.

ZEBRA BOOKS are published by

Kensington Publishing Corp.
850 Third Avenue
New York, NY 10022

First Printing: March, 1996
10 9 8 7 6 5 4 3 2 1

Printed in the United States of America

One

The Earl of Halloway stood, his hands clasped at his back, as he stared out the large panoramic window of his grandmother's drawing room. Its central location afforded a lovely view of the Grange's extensive gardens. Halloway Grange was only one of four Halloway establishments, but it was the only estate that did not belong to the present, young earl. This was because his late grandfather had purchased the estate and deeded it to his young bride as a wedding gift all those years ago. It lay in elegant state only forty minutes out of London and it was where the dowager had come to stay permanently when he died.

The earl smiled ruefully to himself as, it was most certainly, every square foot, all hers, and the earl's very special, very favorite haven. Perhaps that was because his beloved grandmother's strong personality was so entrenched in the Grange. However, he brushed this sentiment aside. It had no place at the moment in his active frenzied mind. He was most frustrated with his grandmother, and not quite certain just what he could do.

A good ten months had passed since Shawna

and Roland had been married. He had thought she had gotten over that. Minnie had seemed pleased enough at their wedding. She had even allowed him more than his usual monthly spending without so much as a frown. His brows drew together over this thought. Something untoward must have gotten her feathers ruffled, for there was no gainsaying that she had since made an about-face and seemed to be on the warpath. She had sent a brief, curt note to him at his bachelor's lodgings. She had made it quite clear that she required him at the Grange to attend her at once. The earl was never one to take orders and he put the note aside, much inclined to ignore her command. However, he was very attached to his grandmother, and she *was* getting on in years. He allowed himself to suffer guilt and conscience, and though he was very much his own man, he discovered that he could not deny her request. Within a short measure of frenzied pacing and mumbled curses, he found himself ordering his man to put together an overnight portmanteau. It wasn't long afterward that, feeling like a schoolboy, that he stood in his grandmother's drawing room, facing her. A sure wariness tickled warning signals in his brain, and he knew he was in for it. He was right.

She took him by storm, getting straight to the point and telling him what she expected of him as a Halloway. She wagged a bony finger at him and advised him that she would no longer allow him to waste his money, his time and his heritage on his road to hell!

He had heard her out in silence. He was in a

sad state. His pockets were to let, he was bored with everything and everyone, and damned sure *he was* on the road to hell. Marriage? His grandmother wanted him safely married and pursuing a respectable life. The very notion made him ill. No, no. Marriage was certainly not a cure for his ills. He sighed over the problem for marriage would solve the financial difficulties he was presently suffering. Still . . . marriage? Waking up to one woman . . . having to do the polite day after day? Having to romance just one woman . . . seeing a hurt look on her face when he couldn't be what she wanted, faithful to one woman? No, not he. He believed a man should be faithful to his wife and he believed he wasn't capable of loving just one woman. He liked too many!

Thus, he and his grandmother had bid one another a very cool good-night before he managed to escape to his room. He had taken breakfast alone in the breakfast parlor and was now just about ready to return to London. The thing was, he believed he had made Minnie unhappy and was irritated by this. He didn't want to leave with things in such a muddle. If he could, he would make one last attempt to smooth things over with his grandmother.

Minerva entered the drawing room to find her grandson deep in thought. He was her darling. He was her dead son's only child. He was also spoiled. She had made him that way with all her petting and attention. He should take his rightful place in the House of Lords. He should direct society, not float about on its outskirts! If he wanted to gamble for a night's entertainment, he should do so in moderation and *not* to pay his overload of debts!

It was time she took control whether he liked it or not, and providence had given her a way.

"Good morning darling," Minnie said softly.

George turned and hazel eyes met hazel eyes. The amber in his eyes glinted with amusement, affection, wariness, "Ah, Grandmama at last." He went to take her outstretched hands and put them to his lips.

She smiled appreciatively, "Charm won't save you lad, I thought I made myself clear last night. I should like your answer before you leave me today."

"My answer is that I shall marry when I am ready, and that may be never. My father and mother were very nearly miserable and they, I am told, were a love match." He shook his head. "I don't know a couple save yourself and grandfather that were comfortable together, let alone happy! If you really mean to cut me off because I am disinclined to make more of a mess of my life than I have already done . . . then do so. It is your choice."

"Cut you off, indeed!" snapped Minnie, "Foolish boy. That is not what I said. And your parents, my dear, were not really a love match. Your mother was a dear sweet child much impressed with your father. He found her beautiful, but they were not suited. I tried to tell your father, but, he was stubborn. Your grandfather prevailed upon me to let it be. Be that as it may, you are wrong. They were not miserable and in fact were quite good friends."

"Marriage is not for me," the Earl said on a low determined note. "So if you mean to cut me— "

"That was not what I said!" snapped his grandmother momentarily irritated.

"What you said, exactly, was that you could no longer stomach my hedonistic exploits and that you would not advance my interest payment for next month."

"Precisely." Minnie nodded.

George was angry with her. It was unthinkable that his inheritance should keep him tied to his grandmother's apron strings. He had turned seven-and-twenty last month. The situation had grown intolerable. His pride however, got the better of him. He inclined his head, "So be it."

"Od's life! Why do you insist on this course? What do you think will happen to you if you marry?"

"It is what would happen to my hapless bride. I should make her wretched." His hand went through his dark locks, "I can not make a woman happy. I can't even make myself happy. You ask too much."

"Do you think so? Well, I think you are made of better stuff than that. We shall see . . ."

He put his arms around his grandmother. "Roland and your dear Shawna will give you great-grandchildren. Now, there is a love match. Shall we watch and see if it lasts past the initial cooing and newness? I doubt it. So, great-grandchildren, that is what you want. Content yourself with that."

"Roland and Shawna have something special. Something beyond the 'cooing and newness,' George. I suppose never having felt it, you must be cynical. You are right, I am well pleased with that match. 'Tis what I always intended."

"Bold-faced fibber!" George was moved to expostulate.

The dowager countess ignored his remark. "What is important is this next season. I am told there are several very lovely ingenues making their entre and— "

"And I don't mean to even look their way."

"Then you shall find yourself without funds and always in debt. I shall not— "

"I know." The earl snapped at her. "You shall not advance me even a sou. You have made yourself quite clear."

"Fine. Then for the moment, we have nothing more to say to one another." Minnie turned her face from him.

The earl sighed sadly. He did not like to leave her this way. He went to her and held her shoulders to drop a kiss on her forehead, "I am sorry I can not please you in this matter, but, you have spoiled me for any other woman. None could measure up to you."

"It isn't me they must measure up to, but you, dearest and one day, one will . . . like it or no."

He kissed her again and was gone. She stood looking out the same window he had been staring out of only moments ago and a soft smile touched her lips. Once again, Minnie had set wheels in motion . . .

Two

Christina Kingsley, known to all as simply, Kitty, was in a sorry frame of mind. Her guardian, who had been father, mother, friend, and dear confident to her since the day she had come to him thirteen years ago, was dead. Death was too well known to Kitty. Death, she had learned when she was five years old, was a final, all encompassing tragedy. Death had orphaned her all those years ago, and now once again, death had taken control.

She had come to her guardian, whom she had learned to call Uncle Edwin, all those years ago, only to watch him grow weak in the end, with an illness that had been a drawn-out, a painful experience for him. Death was something he had welcomed, and though Kitty was relieved that his suffering was over, she was lost in a suffering all her own. Kitty was grieving. No one could ever take his place and for Kitty, there seemed to be no solace whatsoever. She roamed her beloved New Forest in a frenzied and unhappy daze. Nothing seemed to make any sense.

She sat now in a favorite spot deep in the woods. Her sweet chestnut mare was tethered loosely and grazed contentedly nearby. Kitty bent and rubbed her dirt smudged face against her arm as she hugged her knees. She could remember the day she had arrived at Warton Castle. She had been only five years old. She had lost both her parents in a carriage accident, and had not understood why they were gone. She still had a sense of herself as she had stood in the wide long corridor of Warton Castle. There was shining armor and portraits upon portraits of Warton ancestors upon the high walls. She could hear the clanging of footsteps in the hallway and then there he was, a tall man with steel grey hair and dark piercing eyes. He had been her father's best friend. She had always called him uncle, her Uncle Edwin Warton. He had towered above her then and Kitty had clung to her elderly nanny's hand as she watched him, her innocent blue eyes round and wide open with interest.

A moment later, he was bending, picking her up and holding her tightly, robustly declaring, "Kitty. My own little Kitty. You needn't be afraid. You shall never want for anything. Your father was the brother I never had, and you shall be my daughter of the heart!"

So it had been, and now, he too was gone.

Nanny had never approved of Uncle Edwin's behavior. He had been frugal in all things except in the lavish way he had spoiled his Kitty. It was not that he bought her expensive gifts. No, Edwin Warton was known for his tight-fisted manner. He had spoiled her with attention. He taught her to ride, he taught her to hunt. He took her with him on estate business. He took her fishing, sailing. He allowed her every freedom and was pleasantly amused to find her forever in breeches. They were very dear friends.

He had never married and thus, had no children, no sons to carry on for him. He more often than not, thought of Kitty as a son and treated her accordingly. He had adamently refused to allow Kitty to be packed off to a seminary for young ladies, though Nanny begged, and nagged him incessantly on the matter. Thus, Kitty had not been properly schooled in the etiquette of the Beau Monde, but there was none that could ride first flight to hounds as she, or train a pack of hounds as she could. Nanny was not comforted by this, however.

Kitty was very much a hoyden, a laughing, bubbling, teasing and mischievous creature that filled Edwin Warton's home with love. He could not bear to be parted from her and thus, allowed her great license. She was freely given the right to roam the countryside unchaperoned. When Kitty turned eighteen some months ago, Nanny begged her to come to order and behave with more decorum, but Kitty would only laugh.

Towards the end of his life, Edwin Warton realized that his beloved ward was being left at a disadvantage. She had not been taught enough about the society she would have to enter. He had not seen fit to bestow a London Season on her and to make certain she would have a good husband to care for her. He found himself greatly distressed over these facts and then he found a solution.

He had a nephew, his late older sister's only son. He had never really liked her when they grew up together, and had rarely bothered with her after she married. However, there was no denying that she had made an exceptional match when she married the Earl of Halloway's only son and heir. They had produced a son, a robust scamp of a lad, and though Edwin Warton had only seen his young nephew, George, on two or three brief occasions, he had a very vivid memory of the boy as he sat with his pen poised in mid-air. Indeed, in the dim light of his sickroom Warton smiled to think of George. Poor lad, he had lost his father and then his mother, but, there had always been Minerva!

Well, perhaps there was an advantage, a sure advantage in an alliance with this nephew, who had inherited the title of, Earl of Halloway. An earl held position and status in society. The young earl's grandmother, Minerva was a well known and influential Beau Monde hostess. Yes, yes, a definite advantage. Just the ticket for his darling Kitty!

In this frame of mind, he decided the Halloways could be useful and before he died, Kitty's guardian called his solicitor to his sickbed to attend him. Edwin Warton had been a frugal man, with hidden wealth no one save his banker had the least notion about. He carefully made a very calculated alteration to his complicated and thorough will. He then went about the business of writing both to the dowager countess and the earl. Kitty knew nothing about her late guardian's schemes for her future. She only knew that he was gone.

"Kitty." A familiar male voice snapped her out of her daze.

She turned sharply and saw a welcome handsome face. "Harry!" Kitty eyed him up and down. "Well and don't we look the dapper dog." So saying she giggled and sat back on her hands.

He dropped down beside her and pulled her peaked cap off her head. The mantle of long yellow tresses she had tied at the top of her head fell in much disorder round her piquant dirt smudged face.

"Blister it, Kit. You shouldn't be running around in breeches and looking like a ragamuffin. You should have put on a nice gown and presented yourself at church."

Kitty sighed. "Should have, could have, and didn't."

He pulled a face. "Incorrigible child. Look here, Kit, you can't go on grieving forever and you must do something about getting one of your relatives to lend you countenance. You just can't go on alone in the Castle with only your old nanny as a chaperon. It won't do."

"Why?" Kitty grimaced at him.

"Because it just isn't done that way. You are eighteen. Look at you! People always blamed your uncle for letting you run amok. I don't want people pointing in your direction and sniggering. And that is what they will do if you go about dressed no better than a street urchin. I tell you what, madcap, it is time you were presented! Kit, you are a woman full grown and—"

Kitty cut him off, "Do you really think so, Harry? Do you really think I am a woman . . . full grown?" Her eyes twinkled naughtily as she wiggled her shoulders at him in a flirtatious manner, ignoring all the rest. It had always been her philosophy that people would think what they wanted and opinions of strangers did not at all disturb her. She did however, care about what Harry thought. Harry was one-and-twenty, and he had been her knight in shining armor from the first moment they had met. She had been seven, and he had been ten. Their play had always been full of frolic, adventure and good humor and though he was older than she, the odd fact was that it had been Kitty that had ruled their games. He was tall, he was lean, good natured, blond and as blue-eyed as she. More than one resident in the New Forest had often fondly smiled at their public antics and thought that the young heir to Brentwood and Kitty Kingsley were destined for one another in matrimony.

"That won't do my girl and well you know it!" He shook his head and chuckled. "Besides, you don't quite have the knack of it you know."

She put up her chin. "Oh . . . don't I? Well, I suppose that is because Sarah Anne Wrigley does?"

"As a matter of fact, yes. Here have a look." He did his own version of the way Sarah Anne flirted with her shoulder, dipping his own ever so slightly and batting his light colored lashes, *"That,* my girl, is how it is done!"

"Ha! That is how *she* does it." She cocked a look at him, "Now, when and if I choose to use my shoulder to lure a man, I shall do so boldly, as I do everything else!"

He laughed outright. "And even with dirt smudged across your face, your hair a complete mess and in boys' clothing, there is no one I know, not even Sarah Anne Wrigley that can outshine you!"

Kitty blushed happily as she giggled. "Absurd fellow. One minute raking me over the coals and the next filling my head with balderdash."

He chuckled and got to his feet all at once. "Came looking for you zany, because when I stopped by the castle to call on you, your poor old nanny asked me to find you and send you home."

"Did she? But, why so early in the day?" Kitty was surprised.

"Well, and it isn't that early, you know. At any rate, she seemed really anxious." He grinned broadly. "At least, more anxious than usual."

Kitty retrieved her peaked cap from his lap, and almost snorted as she imagined her nanny in a tither. Finding Nanny in a fluster was the norm at the castle. "How *could* you tell?"

Harry did snort, "Years of experience. I've watched her various reactions to your antics over the years, my girl. She only breaks out in hives when you are at your worst."

"Hives? Never say the poor dear has— "

"No, no . . . but, very nearly."

"Well, faith! I wonder what has her bothered now. *I* haven't done anything . . ." Kit caught Harry's dubious expression. "Well, no more than usual, I mean."

"Come on, then. I'll ride along with you and lend you support if you like." Harry was curious for intuition told him that something was towards at the castle.

"Yes, I do like." agreed Kitty as she picked herself up and brushed the grass from her breeches, "It is the price you pay for having found me!"

Three

Nanny was no more than five feet tall. She had a shock of thin short, unruly white hair that she attempted to keep under her mop caps. Her eyes were an unclear shade of grey and very bright. Her nose was pert as was her chin. In spite of her seventy years she was spry, agile, and prided herself on the four miles she managed to walk nearly every day. Kitty, however dear, was a sore trial. Her darling, was the daughter of her heart. She had been there for her since Kitty's birth eighteen years ago, but she had never been able to control her high spirits. Truth was, she didn't really want to. All she wanted was for her Christina to brush out her golden curls, don a pretty gown and take the Beau Monde by storm! It was what her beauty demanded. If only Kitty would cooperate.

Harry was a good boy and would make an excellent country squire one day. Indeed, Nanny would be pleased enough if her Kitty and Harry made a match of it. Well, and where were they? Harry must have found Kit by now. She peered out the wide lead-paned window and immediately saw Kitty and Harry ride their horses round the bend of the long drive and disappear behind the hedges of the stable courtyard.

Hurriedly Nanny left the library behind and charged into the wide austere hall where she proceeded to fold her arms akimbo and pad her feet against the dark oak flooring in a flurry of impatience. Everything she had feared had come to pass. There was nothing more she could do. She had always known they would not be allowed to go on as they were. After all, their positions at Warton were rather vague at best.

It was several moments later that Withers opened the front door to greet his young mistress and her guest. By this time, Nanny's fingers were doing a dance on her upper arms, and she was nearly in tears. Her voice cracked with her emotions, "Well . . . 'tis high time you found her!" Nanny sniffed regally and attempted to maintain her composure.

Harry could see that the elderly woman was much distressed and took this in good stead, saying only, "Indeed."

"I have been worried, my dear, seriously worried." Nanny now directed her piercing glance toward Kitty. "The sky, you know, does not in the least appear friendly and you could have been caught in a nasty storm."

Kit took her nanny's shoulders and dropped a kiss on her nose, "It didn't rain and I *am here*, safe and sound. Now . . . what is it— surely not the weather— that has you at odds?" Kitty cast her a saucy encouraging look meant to pick up her nanny's spirits.

Nanny gave Kitty a quick half smile. "It isn't nice to poke fun when you know how I worry about your running all over the countryside unprotected."

"Dearest," said Kitty, resigned. Nanny was certainly (as Harry had thought) more than usually distressed. "What is it? What is wrong?"

Nanny took both Kitty's hands, "It is Sunday . . . I never expected . . ."

"What love?" Kitty stroked the older woman's arm.

"Mr. Harkins came by today. To see you, dear." There was a portentous sound to her words.

"Mr. Harkins? Uncle's solicitor? Whatever for?"

"Oh, 'tis terrible, terrible," wailed Nanny, who never liked to deal with anything out of the ordinary.

Kitty's eyes opened wide. "Never say we are in debt. Oh Nanny, is it the castle? Do we have to sell the castle to pay Uncle's debts?"

"No, no absurd child!" Nanny scoffed at once. It was obvious Kitty had no understanding of the situation at all. She glanced at Harry and then with a raised brow at Withers who stood quietly in the wings, said, "We had better retire to the library where we may be private." She directed a look toward Harry, "You might as well come along and have it all first hand."

They followed Nanny down the wide corridor to the double doors leading to the huge library Warton Castle boasted. It was a room whose dark oak walls were lined with bookshelves filled with

every possible style of reading material. Its wide
diamond shaped lead-paned windows opened on
to an expansive view of Warton Park. Its furnish-
ings and window hangings were done in rich
brown velvet, trimmed with gold braiding. There
were large carpets of oriental design over the wide
oak planking and an enormous hearth whose
grate forever held a welcoming fire.

Nanny went toward the fireplace, her hands
outstretched toward its warmth. She shook off her
shivers and pulled her dark wool shawl tightly
round her shoulders as she turned to say, " 'Tis
all so very confusing."

"What is, love?" Kitty urged her on.

"Apparently your uncle made a recent, major
change in his will . . ."

"What kind of change?" Harry asked in some
surprise.

"It is about Kitty."

"He changed his will in regard to Kitty?" Harry
asked, eyebrows up. "What kind of a change could
he have instituted?"

"I don't know. Mr. Harkins wouldn't tell me.
He said Christina must be present for the reading
of the will. He said he will return here at four
o'clock."

"Well, what is there in that? Uncle must have
had a good reason to change his will."

Not so naive, Harry and Nanny exchanged
glances. Kitty's father and mother had enjoyed a
comfortable life and had even managed to endow
their daughter with a modest inheritance, with
great emphasis on modest. While Nanny was un-

aware that Warton had been an extremely wealthy man, she had always thought he was a man of respectable means. It had been her hope that she and her dear Christina could at least continue to live at Warton Castle, and that Kitty's guardian might have left Kitty in a position where she might at least be financially secure. A change in Edwin Warton's will set such hopes in limbo. All Nanny could think was that perhaps Kitty had in the end displeased him in some way.

Yet, this could not be so. Nanny was sure of that. Still, worry sets all sorts of hoary notions into motion. What if Edwin Warton had decided his closest male relatives had a very legitimate claim on his estates? Indeed, they did, thought Nanny distractedly. What if these unknown, perhaps very insensitive relatives came and took Warton Castle? Where would she and Kitty go? Would Kitty's competence be enough to hire a modest lodgings? Would Kitty be able to exist in these expensive times? And oh, would Kitty lose her darling horses that she loved so very much?

At that moment nanny jumped to hear Withers who suddenly appeared and announced, "Mr. Harkins."

All eyes turned with some interest to the small, bald fellow that came briskly into the room.

It was an odd coincidence that at that very moment the Earl of Halloway sat back in his winged leather bound chair to read Edwin Warton's letter. The earl was floundering between mixed emotions. His greatuncle's letter had been prefaced with a short note from a Mr. Harkins, who had identified himself as Edwin Warton's solicitor, and briefly advised the earl that his uncle had died leaving him as chief beneficiary of his uncle's considerable fortune.

The earl had only a vague memory of his uncle. There was a pleasant feeling in the memory, nothing more. There was a mild sadness to think that another of his immediate family had died. There was great excitement to discover that his uncle had been rich and that he was now the recipient of that fortune.

The earl had never had the least hint that his uncle Edwin had been a wealthy man. His mother had certainly not spoken of him in such a way. He did recall his grandmother saying once that she could not understand what made his uncle Edwin so miserly. George had simply assumed that his uncle was so because he lived on a limited competence. Well, well, his news was certainly astounding and it was therefore, not surprising that he felt his fingers tremble ever so slightly as he opened his uncle's letter.

Nephew,
It occurs to me that I have neglected you. I should have spent a little more time getting to know you over the years. I beg your pardon. Shall I make up a list of ready excuses? I think not. The truth is, your mother and I were never good friends. There too, she so enjoyed her London. I did not. She loved to flit

amongst the fashionable Beau Monde. I abhorred such a life. For me, Warton Castle, my beloved New Forest, and my fox hounds were all the world I required, especially, you know, after Kitty came to stay.

The earl paused a moment to frown. Kitty? Who was Kitty? He shook his head as no answer came to mind and went on reading.

There it is. Plain speaking, lad, plain speaking. Well, if you are reading this, I'm dead and buried and this is how it stands.

Made myself a fortune out of a more than respectable living. Richer than a Nabob, in fact. My man will give you the details when you come down to Warton Castle. Leaving most of it to you. Plain and simple. However, have a stipulation. You forfeit all if you can't or won't comply with my wishes. There it is, you see. I kept Kitty with me, couldn't bear to send her off to London. That was selfish of me, and I mean to make up for it through your good offices.

Her name is Christina Kingsley. We call her Kitty. She is eighteen years old, and if ever there was a rough and tumble girl, 'tis Kitty. Getting her established in London with your precious Beau Monde won't be easy. But, that is what I require of you. Left Kitty only enough to keep her in comfort. My Kitty doesn't give a fig for fineries. Want her turned out in style, given a London Season . . . two . . . three, whatever it takes to get her married respectably. Now, don't want the fortune hunters after her, so I purposely arranged only a small dowry, just enough. That will sort out the riffraff.

There it is. If you don't take on my ward, see the job through to its completion, Warton Castle and all of my holdings will go to my male next of kin. I would have preferred to leave it all to my Kitty, but she would just go on running wild and never marry if I did, and that would never do.

Good luck, lad . . . it won't be easy.

Edwin Warton

The earl put the letter down on his well-used oak desk. His eyebrows were up and his hazel eyes were lit with amber lights. Fire and Hell! Why was it every time a fortune was offered to him, there was marriage attached. He sighed heavily and conceded to himself that at least *he* wasn't expected to marry the chit. Damn, but his uncle's last words were, "it won't be easy." Perfect. She no doubt was a wretched looking thing. And with only a small dowry, what hope was there? What to do? What did he know about bringing out an ingenue? He would need to open Halloway House in Kensington Square. He would need a respectable hostess. His grandmother came to mind and his eyes narrowed. Had she known about this? Od's life! He was very certain that she had known about this yesterday morning when he had left her at the Grange. Sly thing. Well, well, he would stop by and pay her a call on his way to the New Forest, for one thing was for certain, this fortune was not one he was about to allow to slip through his fingers!

Four

Mr. Harkins had read, and thoroughly explained the meaning of Edwin Warton's will. It secretly boded ill with him that he could not give a full accounting to Miss Kingsley of her personal holdings. He had however, advised her that he would be happy to do so after her London Season, when he hoped he would be able to congratulate her. This he had said with a cough into his fist and a flush on his cheeks before he took his leave and hurried off.

He had been gone for some ten minutes leaving behind the occupants of the library in deep thought. It was Kitty who finally dispelled the stillness of the room by jumping out of her chair, to defiantly state, "Well, I won't go. No one can make me." Her blue eyes glinted the truth to her words.

"Dear child, it was your guardian's dying wish." nanny chided her softly. She was taken aback by the conditions of Warton's will, but not entirely overset by it.

Kitty softened. "Yes, but I don't know this Earl of Halloway. If he is uncle's real nephew why have we never seen him? Why was there never any mail from him?" She stomped her foot. "I don't want to go to London for a Season, Nanny, I wouldn't know how to . . . to manage surrounded by high flyers, and I *don't* want to get married!" Kitty looked to Harry for help. "This will is absurd. I can't be made to go to London, can I? No one can force me to marry?"

Harry shook his head as he moved to pat the top of her messy blond curls. The thing was, Harry was more than a trifle confused by this new development. Kitty's guardian had contrived an unexpected and a most irregular will. He had never heard its like. On the one hand, it was just what Kitty needed. A London Season was precisely what his unselfish Kit deserved. She should certainly be tricked out in fashionable gowns, suitable jewels and female finery. He had often thought so, but the truth was Kitty should have also been given some fashion sense and fashion etiquette long ago. Yes, she should be taken to London and, yes, she should be introduced to the ton. It was her right as a Kingsley. She should be taken to the theater, to routs, and balls. She should be introduced to eligible bachelors. The thing was, Kitty had not been properly prepared for the all powerful ton. She wasn't familiar with their rules and edicts. She would frown on the ton's penchant for on-dits and gossip. She really would not understand society's subtlies. She knew nothing about the Beau Monde, and there was no doubt in his mind that Kitty could so easily be hurt.

"No," Harry finally decided to answer in cautious terms. "You can not be *made* to *honor* your late guardian's wishes."

Kitty's mouth dropped as the impact of Harry's words penetrated to her heart and she wrung her hands. "Oh, oh, this is dreadful. Dear Uncle Edwin. Why did he do this? For me? He thought he was doing this for my sake. I know. How ungrateful it would be if I ignored his last wish." She turned then in some desperation to her nanny, and with a sudden choking sound dove into her nanny's arms.

"There, there child. It will not be so bad." Nanny soothed.

"What won't be so bad?" a familiar male voice rallied from the doorway.

Kitty sniffed to find the young squire, Clayton Bickwerth, standing in the doorway. There was nothing unusual in that. The tall handsome fellow had been very nearly a fixture at Warton Castle for some months, coming and going with great familiarity.

He shot a wide grin at Harry and went forward to receive both of Kitty's hands, noting that she stood in all her dirt as usual, all hoyden. She was, he thought to himself, at least amusing. He swung her hands a bit and winked down at her, urging a smile to her full lips. There was no doubt that she had been crying for the dirt on her cheeks was tear stained and streaked.

Harry watched them, a frown settling on his face. Clay was a friend, of sorts. They had been at Cambridge together, though Clay was a year older. They had often enjoyed hunting beside one another in the field, roaring with laughter as they took their fences together, riding neck or nothing in first flight. They had met one another for a night's entertainment at the Red Bull more often than not, and Harry had to admit that he had always enjoyed Clay Bickwerth's company. Still, Clay's sudden and obvious interest in Kitty had only begun when Edwin Warton had taken to his sickbed five months ago. This had Harry more than a little disturbed. There too, the fact was, Kit wasn't in Clayton's usual style. And, Harry knew that the word was, the young squire was in pecuniary straits. This was due to the fact that his late father had run up a number of debts during his flamboyant lifestyle, most of which had been spent amongst the ton in London. The young squire had been forced to take a mortgage on his estate, and there was no doubt whatsoever, in order to come about, he would have to make a financially advantageous marriage.

"Uncle Edwin's will was just read to us." Kitty explained to the newcomer. "It seems I have to leave Warton and allow some stranger to take me off to London." Kit was attempting to put on a brave face, but no one in the room was fooled.

Clayton Bickwerth pulled a face. "Packed off to London? With strangers? What strangers? Why?" He didn't like this, for it did not fit in with his plans.

Ah, thought Harry, now we shall see a retreat! Clay needed to marry someone with more than just a comfortable portion. This would change everything. He didn't think Kit had lost her heart to Clayton yet, but, if the man had persisted, there was no telling, and Harry didn't want Kitty's pure young heart broken. No doubt, Clayton would now take himself out of the running.

"Uncle Edwin has a nephew, his real heir, and as I am only his ward he must have felt it only right to leave him the Castle and the bulk of his estate. The odd thing is, he created a stipulation. Everything goes to his nephew, providing he takes me to London, and arranges for me to have a proper Season, with marriage at its conclusion." Kit made a face as she moved away from Clayton toward Harry. "You see I am left with no choice, but to honor my guardian's dying wish, so I suppose that I must go, but I detest the thought."

"Never mind, madcap. You will set London on its ears." Harry said touching her pert nose and winning a half smile from her.

Clayton frowned. "Do you mean that this heir only inherits if you marry?"

"That is the long and the short of it, I suppose," said Kitty clucking her tongue.

Clay said nothing to this but stood lost to his quick cogitations. To Harry the young squire's thoughts were completely transparent. Nanny made a decision and started wagging a finger at her charge. "That is quite enough, my dear. Time enough for such speculation. What you need now, right now, is a bath and a change of clothing."

A footman appeared with a tea tray laden with an assortment of small cakes, bread, jam and fresh butter.

"Oh," said Kitty realizing she was famished, "Tea, Nanny, you can not send Clay and Harry off without refreshments, and I might as well have my tea while it is hot."

"Very well, as you will. I have always believed tea helps in all matters." sighed Nanny who began to pour.

The earl looked up at the sky. He didn't bother taking out his pocket watch. He could see by the position of the slightly obscured sun that it was past late afternoon. He brought his snowy grey to a complete stop in the middle of the country Post Road. Here he waited patiently for some minutes until he caught sight of his new chocolate brown barouche, a prize he had won in a game of chance. He had only the expense of having the doors painted with the Halloway crest. However, the smile this memory brought was only momentary and he was soon sighing with sure weariness. As smart as the new barouche was, it also was certainly slowing the pace of the journey to the New Forest, but really, what choice did he have? He needed this equipage if he was going to escort Miss Kingsley and her duenna to London. The thought of this project made him moan out loud. His grandmother had been suspiciously gracious and accepted to go on ahead to Halloway House and have it opened and ready for their arrival. However, he could only assume that his grandmother was lonely now that her ward, Shawna, was married and busy running about the country with her husband, Roland. The notion of his grandmother playing hostess for him in the town house brought mixed emotions. He loved her and was happy to provide her with a measure of happiness, but she was a strong willed woman and he would have to be wary of her wiles. Damn! This whole thing was a nuisance. He shook his head and looked down the road at his approaching carriage. It had been his choice to take to saddle and ride his snowy grey gelding on this journey. The young gelding was only four years old and full of lively spirits. He dearly needed the fidgets worked out of him. However after some five hours, most of which had been spent keeping his horse to a walking pace, he was saddle sore and road weary. With a long intake of air that he immediately blew out, he stood high in his stirrups, giving his muscles a much needed stretch. His young gelding was hanging his head, much tired as well. He smiled as he bent to pat the animal's snowy neck again, "Well done, Prancer. Well done, indeed."

Again he looked to his coach and mumbled to himself, "Come along, Max, don't be all day, move, move them up . . . come along." He watched his driver bring up his handsome matched bays. Max was his head groom, a reformed street make-bait, and one of his two most valued servants. The other was Luts, the earl's valet, who was very nettled at being left behind on this journey. The earl was considered a Corinthian, a top sawyer, the very pink of the ton, and

Luts took great pride in dressing and attending to the earl's wardrobe. The earl's athletic form allowed Luts great license for the earl looked perfect in everything he wore. Luts only concern was the fact that the handsome earl cared little about his appearance. Perversely, the earl's cavalier attitude regarding his clothing quite helped to make him and his little valet the heart of the Beau Monde's fashionable center. Much to the earl's considerable surprise and his valet's satisfaction, he soon discovered that he was held second only to Brummell himself. Luts sighed to think the earl might not care and neglect to have his boots properly shined while he was not about to see to this extremely important duty. However, there was nothing for it, Luts quite understood that he was needed in London to attend to the exciting occupation of packing the earl's latest and best clothing and belongings for the short journey from the earl's lodgings to his town house.

At the moment, the earl was unconcerned about the dust on his riding coat and boots. He was quite happy to have his beaver top hat low and rakisly set on his head as it had kept the sun from his eyes most of the day. He only knew that he was greatly fatigued and wearily advised his animal,

"I tell you what, Prancer old boy, we've been good, you and I. That's right. We deserve a respite. Soon, very soon it will be water and hay for you and brandy and sirloin for me, I do promise you."

Prancer seemed to think this was fair, for he

nodded his head vigorously and released a heavy, wet snort. The earl laughed and as his driver was pulling up the matched bays to a stop not far off, called, "Well then, Max, I'm going up ahead to the Red Lion. It is dinner and relaxation for all of us."

Max had been with the earl any number of years. He served in many capacities, chiefly as the earl's head groom. When the earl had found him, he had been a half starved orphan living by his wits in the streets of Soho. This time, his wits had not saved him and he had been caught in the act of stealing food. A local beadle had cuffed him and would have dragged him away had the earl not seen the whole and taken pity. The earl had been just about twenty at the time; Max had been no more than twelve. The earl had paid for the food and taken young Max to his grandmother's stables at Halloway Grange. He left the boy there, giving him instructions to learn all he could about horses. Max would have done anything the earl had asked, but was lucky enough to find he had a liking for horses and a quiet skill with them as well. The Earl often looked in on his protege while visiting with his grandmother and encouraged him along. By the time the earl had turned one-and-twenty, Max was with him and loving every minute of his employment. Max had just turned nineteen years old, and was given all the liberties of a trusted and beloved servant. Hence, the rivalry between Luts and Max.

"Aye, m'lord. Been hopin' ye might be thinkin' along sech fine lines," said young Max with a grin.

"Impudent fellow," laughed the earl as he rode on ahead.

Five

Morning came for both the earl and Kitty in a blaze of sunshine. April had arrived nattily attired. All the signs of spring had begun. The green stalks of daffodils were already covering ground, sprouting their blooms with a hint of yellow flowers. Crocus in varieties of purples and white flowers looking like miniature tulips had escaped their landscaped beds and abounded prettily in nearby grassy fields. Trees everywhere were vibrant with new red buds. The season showed promise of being fruitful.

In addition to the glorious morning, a convivial evening with a party of young bloods much like himself, had done a great deal to restore the earl's sense of well being. A pretty barmaid not adverse to a harmless kiss or two, went a long way to ease his tension. Thus, the earl was able to enjoy (though albeit, with a heavy head) the scent of fresh spring air as he took to horse. In a few hours they would reach Lyndhurst, in the New Forest and his newly inherited estate, Warton Castle. Newly inherited estate? Well, damn, he answered himself, it would be when he fulfilled his part!

He had made up his mind during the night, that he was not going to trouble himself with this Kingsley girl. After all, launching an ingenue was not the job of an acknowledged rake. Since his grandmother seemed to enjoy the notion of taking a role once again amongst the Beau Monde, he would allow her to do so completely. He would leave the chit in his capable grandmother's hands. He could do no better for if anyone could get a girl paired off and safely wed, it was Minnie! Of course, he supposed he would have to put in an appearance. Yes, he would escort them to a few balls and such, perhaps, even to Almacks, but more than that could not possibly be required of him. With any good luck, Minnie would find the chit a husband in her first season, and *that* would be that!

In this frame of mind the earl was able to shrug off his irritation and discover the beauty of a fine spring day as he jogged his horse along the country road. Max some distance at his back had grave doubts about this entire affair. Speaking gravely to the matched bays sedately pulling the equipage along, he gave them his considered opinion. "Oi don't know about all this. This is out of course. Not m'lord's ken looking out for some flash piece of fluff? Lor, but we be in for a time that's whot Oi be thinkin'."

The earl, calm in the belief he had arrived at a reasonable conclusion to his problem, gave no more thought to Miss Kingsley. He hadn't the slightest reservation about her compliance with his plans. After all, he could not imagine any young, countrified female with little prospects who would not wish to make an advantageous marriage for herself.

However, that certainly was the case. Kitty had not spent a restful night. She had risen from her bed earlier than usual, whereupon she dove into her comfortable breeches and jogged down to the stables. There in the quiet dawn she saddled her pretty chestnut mare and took her into the clear spring breeze. She had to think. She had to find a way out of this tangle her guardian had set in motion. She didn't want to go to London, and she didn't want to get married. Kitty wanted things to remain as they were. Change was such a frightening undertaking, especially a change of this magnitude.

Kitty pulled her horse up before the stone wall between the farmer's wide grassy fields and sighed unhappily. She was out of temper, she was frustrated, she was at a loss for an acceptable solution to her problem, and she was certainly feeling guilty. How ungrateful of her to feel and behave this way. Her guardian's dying, his *dying* wish was something she could not ignore. She was being so selfish, wanting her own way. Yes, but, she just couldn't get married . . . at least not yet. She wasn't ready. She couldn't imagine what it would be like to have to always wear fancy gowns and do the pretty at London routs. She was very sure she would not fit in. She was only a country girl with country manners. She was used to eating her dinner at five o'clock and getting out of bed just after dawn. Everything would be different, and she was very sure she would not enjoy the change. There would be no more breeches and racing across the fields. There would be no more fishing. There would be no more . . . Harry.

A large tear formed and spilled over and then she heard her name. "Fie zany! What's towards?"

"Oh, Harry. It is dreadful. Dreadful. How shall I get on without you? Life in London will be a misery," cried Kitty soulfully.

Harry reached over and patted her roughly on her delicately small shoulder. "Plucky girl, the truth is you get on very well without me. Always have. You'll do."

"This is different, Harold," sniffed the lady feeling he did not properly understand. "Everyone will be a stranger."

He shrugged. "Never stopped you before, Kit my girl." He grinned at her, "I mean, you aren't claiming to be shy?"

She grimaced at him. "You haven't the least bit of sensibility."

"Kit— "

"Never mind." She cut him off as she took her horse round, walking him away from the wall and then turning him some paces from it to face it once more. "Are you coming?"

He laughed out loud as he followed suit. "What do you think, Miss Kingsley?"

Laughing they took their horses over the wall, cantered the next field where Harry tipped his hat to her as he took his leave. "Thank you, Miss Kingsley for an enjoyable ride. I look forward to

a time when we may do this again." He grinned
boyishly with an inclination of his head. "There,
town manners, nothing to it. Answer me in kind."

She laughed and regally arched a look. "I don't
do the polite with friends . . . no point." She
smiled naughtily at him.

He laughed. "I tell you what, zany, throw answers like that about at the ton, and you'll do very
well!"

She giggled. "But, I don't want to do very well.
I want to stay here. I don't want to be tested by
the ton."

"Incorrigible." he laughed as he started off,
turned once more to wave at her and vanished
behind a bend in the road.

Some hours later, Kitty stepped out of Mrs.
Cribbins kitchen, turned to wave again, and un-
tethered her horse. She was feeling much better
after their cozy visit, (accompanied as it was with
sweet buns and hot tea). Farmer Cribbins was one
of Warton's tenant farmers. Long ago Mrs. Cribbins had taken Kitty under her motherly wing,
and a fond relationship often sent Kitty in that
direction when she was troubled.

Mrs. Cribbons had sipped her tea and listened
quietly as Kitty wailed over her woes. However,
when Kitty had stopped and finally asked for an
opinion, Mrs. Cribbons had pursed her lips,
arched her thick dark brows and folded her hands
in her lap. "Ye are not going to loke what I 'ave
to say to ye, child."

"That never stopped you before," teased Kit
with a twinkle in her lovely blue eyes.

Mrs. Cribbins smiled sweetly. "Aye then. Loke it or no, yer dear guardian set a task fer ye. Might as well brace yerself, 'coz the way I see it, ye ain't getting no choice."

Kitty had sighed. "I suppose when all is said and done, Mrs. Cribbins, that is the sore truth."

"Aye, so it is . . ." Mrs. Cribbins had softly answered. Now, as Kitty rode away, she could hear the words again. Well, that was that, she would just have to resign herself. She turned her horse onto the Post Road and headed for home. It wasn't long before she came upon a handsome chocolate brown equipage broken down in the middle of the road. Its young driver was bent over the wheel. He looked up to find a gamin of a girl in boy's clothing and wearing a boy's peaked cap approach.

Max's jaw dropped as he watched her nimbly jump out of her saddle and call out, "Hallo. Do you need some help?"

"Ay, but, none that ye can give me." Max grinned condescendingly.

Kitty did her own inspection of the lopsided wheel, and pointed. "You need a new bolt there, nothing more."

"Aye, that Oi do and Oi carry a spare wit me, but thing is, Oi can't be lifting the wheel and putting the bolt in place all at the same time, now can Oi?" retorted Max on a superior note.

"Lucky for you, sir," bantered Kit, "that I happened along. You lift, I'll manage the bolt."

"Ha! Whot then, Oi'd get two yards Oi would

and bam, the bolt would be gone again. Ye ain't got brawn enough to do it up right," Max scoffed.

"No, perhaps I do not. However, once it is on, you can release the wheel and tighten the thing to your satisfaction. What say you?" Kitty offered with a warm smile.

Max considered this. With a nod of approval he said, "Aye then, we'll give it a go." So saying he produced the spare bolt, handed it to Kitty and proceeded to lift the wheel and shift it into place. This done he ordered, "Go on then, girl."

Kitty smiled at his form of address, but slipped the bolt on and tightened it as best she could. "There. It's all yours now. Good luck." Kit turned and started for her horse who was contentedly grazing along the road.

"Oi'm grateful, halflin'." Max called out as he watched her mount.

"Good." Kitty laughed, "Mayhap you'll smile the next time we chance to meet." So saying she rode past him, hurrying her pace, for by now Nanny would be ready with a wagging finger!

The earl sat on his horse at a complete stop just at the signpost that led to Warton Castle. He did not want to turn off the main road until he was certain Max was close behind. More than a few minutes had already passed by and with a thoughtful frown, the earl started back down the road in search of his carriage.

Kitty was riding her horse at a gallop for she

knew she was late and saw no one to worry about ahead. However, just then, the earl rounded the blind bend in the road, and his young gelding started at the sudden emergence of another steed. The earl, who after several hours in the saddle was relaxing his leg, was caught off guard and nearly unseated. As he recovered himself, Kitty slowed to apologize, but before she could utter the words, she heard him thunder, "What in blazes do you think you are doing, you damn fool?"

Kitty's chin went up. "Riding my horse, sir. And you?" She could see that though he was dusty, he was certainly what Harry would call a top sawyer, however her temper was already on the loose.

The earl took a second look and realized that the urchin was female. However, he was still irritated at having lost his seat, more so now that it was a young woman who had witnessed his transgression, "Is that what you call it, riding?" He returned derisively.

"Indeed I do, but, judging by your style, I can see why you do not!" retorted the lady, gathering her mare in hand. Kitty often was guided by impulse. Running along the side of the road was a ditch with a wall a little behind. Her mare realized what her mistress wanted of her and came to attention. In very fine style, Kitty trotted her chestnut over the ditch, took a pace and went over the fence with a happy laugh.

As angry as the earl felt at her behavior, he could not help but admire her management of the in and out. However, he was not in the mood. He had to find Max and make the last leg of the journey to Warton Castle.

Six

"So!" Nanny was tapping her little foot and her arms were folded across her chest. "You have decided to come home, have you?"

Kitty hurried across the library carpet and took Nanny's diminutive shoulders in hand. "Don't scold, Nanny. It's too lovely a day to be cross with me." She sealed her words with a fond kiss on her nanny's cheek.

Nanny was not mollified and was not about to be put off so easily on this particular occasion. She sniffed to say, "Tch, tch, not this time, my girl, not this time! Don't you realize that, I am here, living in dread, ever since Mr. Harkins advised us yesterday that he had forwarded letters to both the Earl of Halloway and his grandmother, the dowager Countess of Halloway. Don't you realize they will be upon us any moment? Don't you know what they will say to me if they find you like *that?*" Her hands waved at Kitty's breeches.

"We live in the country. I am not canvassing the world dressed in breeches, only when I ride out on my own land, after all."

"That is just that. Now, we know this is not your own land," wailed Nanny.

"Well, that is a truth. But, Uncle did say I should live here until I am married, so— "

"What is there in that?" Nanny returned in shocked accents, "You are eighteen years old. You must be brought out. You can not run wild in breeches! What will they think of me, these Halloways? What will they say?"

"You are the best nanny in all the world," Kitty answered with a defiant look.

"They will not think so. And they would be right. They would think me irresponsible."

"No one shall attack you or your abilities while I am about." retorted Kitty staunchly, "But, if you like, I will go up right now, bathe and put on a pretty gown."

"My dearest child," cooed Nanny giving Kitty's cheek an affectionate pinch.

The library door opened and Withers announced in awe, "The Earl of Halloway!"

Nanny's small aged hand went to her forehead and she showed signs of swooning. "We are undone!"

"Hush love," whispered Kitty taking charge of the situation. "Here sit, go on, sit," Kitty placed her nanny in a nearby chair of maroon damask and straightened up. "I shall handle this Earl of Halloway. Just relax."

The earl strode through the double doors, past Withers, and stopped abruptly to take stock of his surroundings. His large, impressive lines seemed to fill the room and for a fraction of a moment no one spoke. As Withers withdrew, quietly closing the doors, Kitty found her voice and ejaculated, *"You!"*

The earl quickly realized he was being addressed by the little termagant he had just encountered on the road. His expressive dark brow rose and a decided sneer curved his fine lips, "Indeed, and apparently at a disadvantage. You now know who I am." He inclined his uncovered dark head of curls. "But, I do not have the slightest notion who you may be." The insult was there, and Nanny nearly gasped.

"Christina Kingsley, my lord," said Kitty at once, her chin well up. She turned to wave to her nanny. "And this is Miss Diddles." Kit was in a white heat and when thusly afflicted she was well able to hold her own. She cast him a bold once over, "I can see by your road dust that you have been traveling for a great length of time, my lord. No doubt, you must be, er, looking forward to a nice hot bath." She was showing him as best she could who ruled the roost at Warton. Breeches or no, she meant for him to behave respectfully to her and hers. "If you will excuse me, I will see our housekeeper and make the necessary arrangements. In the meantime, please relax by the fire. I will have tea brought to you momentarily." So saying she moved towards the door, pausing there to incline her head. "And if you like, there is a very fine brandy on the sideboard." So saying she turned on her heel and, in all her stable dirt, regally attempted to leave the earl at her back.

"Touché!" Halloway inclined his head, "I would tip my hat to you, however, *I* did not wear it into your home." He was of course referring to the fact that she was wearing a weathered wool cap under which all (though he could not see it) her glorious blond hair was hidden.

Kitty's temper soared and her bright blue eyes fairly sparkled as she mockingly clapped her hands. "How very proper and mannerly of you, my lord." A sad sigh. "I am ever so remiss at such manners." Her sigh was a show of affectation and this time she did leave the room with her nanny gasping near to swoon at her back.

Halloway stiffened, winning his inheritance was going to be more of a chore than he had imagined. He doubted that even his elegant grandmother could make a silk purse out of this little sow. Damn, but, she was more hoyden than he had thought possible. He turned to find Miss Diddles nervously pinching at her dark shawl, and softened at once. Smiling in the woman's direction, he moved toward the brandy decanter said kindly, "Well, Miss Diddles, am I correct in assuming you have been with Miss Kingsley most of her life?"

"Indeed, from the moment she was born. I have been her nanny." She smiled sweetly. "I suppose that is what I still am, 'tis what Kitty has always called me." She wanted to offer him some sort of explanation for Kitty's clothing and very nearly offensive behavior, but thought better of it and held her tongue.

"Ah, Kitty is it?" Under his breath he said, "With sharp claws, I see." Then once more with a smile added, "May I pour you a little madeira while we wait for tea?"

Nanny rarely indulged but she was so agitated that she fluttered. "Oh . . . oh . . . I . . . well . . . yes, please."

He smiled kindly at her as he handed her a glass of the light wine. "Drink hardy, Miss Diddles. I know this unusual situation has us all overset."

In this, the earl had grossly understated the matter. He may have been irritated at suddenly being the caretaker of a wild rude child, however, he at least had a goal worthy its effort. Kitty on the other hand, had no such goal and was in a fury of frustration. She had no choice but to adhere to her guardian's dying wishes. She was faithful to love, to what was right, but she was supremely unhappy. She stomped about the house, threw her prized cap against the wall and stood in the large, well-ordered kitchen and demanded of no one in particular, "Tell me if you can, just how am I going to allow that arrogant, cold hearted, self-serving, over-bearing blade to take me off to London?" She had not expected any of the startled, but concerned staff to reply and ranted on, "It won't work," Kitty now directed her comment to their large apple-cheeked cook as she stamped out of the room. "I shan't go!" she advised the footman at the top of the stairs, "He is completely insufferable!" She told her bedroom door, and then once within the quiet of her room and facing the truth as she stared at her bed, Kitty burst into tears!

* * *

Clayton Bickwerth reined in his chestnut hunter and waited. He could see a young woman in a dark brown riding habit and top hat was slowly riding her roan toward him from the intersecting sandy country road. He knew just who she was and had thought until recently, he would not have to resort to this. Damn, but, she was ham handed with the reins! Someone had evidently taught her how to sit a side saddle neatly, but had neglected to show her how to protect her poor horse's mouth. He resigned himself, and looked her over. Well, at least her figure was trim. She was nearly upon him, and he felt a moment's panic and an urge to ride off. However, he put on his most charming smile and quietly moved his horse towards her. Egad, if ever there was a dour-faced, straight-nosed creature, it was Miss Henrietta Harkins. He tipped his hat to her, allowing his eyes to stroke her as though she were a work of art.

Young Bickwerth's tastes did not run along Henrietta's lines. She, on the other hand, thought him with his tall frame, and his sandy hair, a veritable Adonis. Henrietta was one-and-twenty. The young squire was not much older, but, to the reticent Henrietta, he seemed a sophisticated man of the World. She had not yet been able to ensnare a man, a fault her mother was forever whispering in her ear. She was beginning to think that in spite of her sizable inheritance, this particular feat was beyond her limited skills. Henrietta was a good-hearted, dear, warm, sweet-natured creature. When amongst friends such as Kitty or Harry, she was full of wit, wisdom and laughter. However, all these characteristics submerged in fear when she found herself in the company of strangers, especially when that company was made up of the opposite sex. An overwhelming shyness would take total control of her, as it did now when she tried to raise her soft brown eyes to Clayton Bickwerth's face.

As the handsome squire smiled and tipped his hat to her, she felt herself color and found her conversation lost in a series of absurd giggles. She further embarrassed herself for her reaction to this was to clamp her fine kid gloved hand tightly over her small mouth making her nearly choke. Bickwerth's eyes widened, but immediately took command of the situation with polite conversation. "Hallo, dear Miss Harkins. How fortunate I count myself today. I don't normally take this road at this time of day. So, there is something to be said for spontaneity. My break with routine has won me a worthy prize!"

Henrietta felt dizzy with the compliment. What should she say? She blushed brightly and managed, "How kind."

"So I would count it, if you allowed me to accompany you?" What did the bright Kitty see in this drab creature? To be sure, they were often found laughing in one another's company. At any rate, Miss Harkins was an heiress to an immense fortune. In light of his present circumstances he had no choice but to pursue her in earnest. He looked her over once more and mastered a shudder. Her father was a brilliant solicitor, and the third son of a baron. Her mother was the fourth daughter of an earl. The alliance had been frowned upon, but allowed. However, he-knew that both Henrietta's parents wanted her to marry a title, and enter the heady world of the Beau Monde. This became a genuine possibility when Henrietta's maternal aunt had died and left her enormous wealth to her favorite niece. Right then, a marriage of convenience. It was, after all, the accepted mode of their class. Once married, he would have her fortune and happily, easily, without guilt, go his own way. Still, he had hoped he could have married a woman he at least found attractive? This, by Jove, this certainly was *not* what he had planned!

Seven

Kitty surveyed herself in the oak framed long looking glass. Nanny had brushed Kitty's golden tresses until they fairly glistened, and then tied them at the top of Kitty's head with a blue satin ribbon. Thick wispy curls formed bangs over her forehead, and short golden curls shadowed her pretty ears. A blue satin ribbon showed to advantage Kitty's fine neck. Kitty could not say why, but she had chosen to wear her favorite dinner gown for her first formal encounter with the earl. It was a simple creation of light blue muslin dotted throughout with soft white. Its neckline was too high to be thought provocative and it was trimmed with a simple white lace fringe. Its long sleeves were puckered at the shoulder, tight fitting along her slender arms, and trimmed with the same lace at the wrists. The gown's fitted waist was banded with a wide sash of blue satin that matched the satin round her neck. Her low slippers were of blue satin. Kitty had liked this gown when she purchased it some six months ago, but now, scanning herself, she was quite dissatisfied. She frowned at her image which looked no more than fourteen. Everything about her appearance was demure. All at once, a notion clicked in Kitty's brain. If London and the Beau Monde were her destination, then she would take them on, and *this* was not the image she would present.

She turned to Miss Diddles and pulled a face. "Do you know what Nanny, this will never do in London. Henrietta was with me when I chose it and I remember she wrinkled her nose and said that she *supposed* it would do for the country. At the time, I didn't understand what she meant. Now, though, I quite see. Henrietta has an eye for such things, and she is very well versed in fashion for you know she has already suffered two London Seasons!"

Nanny sniffed. "Well as seasoned as Miss Harkins may be, the fact of the matter, my girl, is that you are presently here, in the country, and your gown looks very nice on you."

Kitty frowned at her reflection. "I don't want to look *very nice*. If the Beau Monde prize's fripperies over all else, then I must get the hang of dressing far smarter than nice. Otherwise, the ton will eat me up and spit me out. I don't want that to happen to me. I don't want to return home with my head down and my spirit broken."

"Spit you out? What kind of talk is that for a lady? Kitty, you must learn to watch your wayward tongue. As for all the rest, really, I doubt that anyone could break *your* spirit, my love," Nanny replied with feeling.

Kitty laughed, "Well, they could, if I let them. And if they are all like the earl. Faith, Nanny, I will never take, *never,* because he dislikes me as much as I dislike him."

Nanny sighed sadly. "The thing is, it was so unfortunate that he happened in on you while you were wearing those dreadful clothes." She shook her head over the problem. "For my part, I found him all that was gentlemanly and kind."

"Did you?" Kitty retorted in some surprise. "I tell you, Nanny, he is nought but a rogue. Arrogant, conceited, overbearing, and no doubt, a libertine as well!"

"Oh, that can't be true. Your guardian would not have put you in the hands of a . . . a libertine," objected Nanny reasonably. Kitty gave this a moment's thought. "Well, Uncle had not seen the earl in many years."

"Come, child, we are going to be late for dinner, and that would never do," said Nanny taking Kitty's hand and moving hurriedly toward the bedroom door, thus, putting an end to a line of conversation that was sure to lead into dangerous territory.

The earl had bathed and changed his clothing. He wore a sky blue superfine cutaway, short-tailed as befitting his country surroundings. His waistcoat was white embroidered with blue silk, and his breeches were soft textured buff colored buckskins. It was obvious that his ensemble had come from a tailor of the first stare. It was also obvious that while the earl's style was certainly high fashion, there was nothing of the dandy about him.

His height was mountainous, his shoulders broad, his waist trim and his thighs athletic. His cravat, though tied with precision and neatness, had not the finesse of the beau. The earl's other enviable attributes were boldly striking. His dark, neck-length hair tinged with auburn was cut à la Brutus, and his green flecked hazel eyes were alert.

He sipped his brandy slowly as he stood, one elbow leaning against the fireplace mantle as he awaited his young hostess and her nanny who, since she was to dine with them, seemed more of a companion. What a devilish situation he was in to be sure, he thought. Warton Castle, its lands, its estates, his uncle's vast fortune were all his, and yet, not quite. There was the damnable stipulation of the will. His future was evidently dependent on one thing. He would have to find an acceptable husband for a termagant of a female, a wild unruly hoyden with no manners and no style. Thunder and turf, a job indeed!

These depressing cogitations were momentarily put aside as the door opened wide and Nanny, almost on tiptoes, gingerly stepped through, closely followed by Miss Kingsley. The earl's expressive dark brows went up and his hazel eyes opened wide. The light stepping little fairy creature that had just entered the room was a spritely blond. Her pretty, pixie-like countenance bore no resemblance whatsoever to the girl he had met earlier. Her figure, even in her schoolgirl dress, was most intriguing. And her eyes . . . such incredible, such invitingly warm blue eyes. Could this possibly be the same little spitfire, the shrew, he had met in the afternoon?

Kitty nodded politely for she was determined to be civil as she said on a cool note, "My lord."

He held his brandy glass to her and smiled. "Ah, Miss Kingsley, I take it?" The inference was there, clear and biting, as he followed it up with, "Better, my dear, better."

The earl's casual words stung sharply and once again Kit was on her mettle. Her chin went up as she quietly retorted, "Ah, no doubt, high praise indeed from a London dandy."

Miss Diddles nearly swooned as she gasped, "Christina!"

No one, not a soul in his lifetime had ever thought of the earl as a dandy. He was momentarily bereft of speech, but made a quick recovery. "From a London dandy, I don't suppose you would have had even that much, Miss Kingsley. From me, however, it was no more, no less than what it was. I meant only that you look better out of your dirt." He eyed her from suddenly brooding eyes. The chit had certainly taken him in dislike. No matter, he didn't give a jot for that. At least she had countenance. That should help to get her married off. Countenance, a respectable portion and his grandmother's good offices.

Kit felt her cheeks grow hot. To be fair to the man, she had certainly not presented a genteel appearance that afternoon. She knew her gown was dowdy in design and certainly not suitable for a London drawing room. However, Kitty's temper had been stirred and fairness had nought to do with the workings of her agitated mind. "So I look better, but not quite to your sophisticated tastes?"

"My tastes have nought to do with it. However," he inclined his head and gave her a gentle smile that almost, not quite, but almost, won a smile from her in return, "if you wish to feel comfortable amongst your own while in London, and enjoy a successful Season, we will have to see to your wardrobe." The earl had not the slightest notion that he was offering offense to a proud young lady. Kitty appeared to him to be no more than a child, a country child who needed guiding. While he had no intention of taking on that job personally, he was not adverse to offering his advice. After all, he was playing for high stakes.

"I don't give a fig about fashions and I don't give a fig about a successful London Season." Kitty was totally out of control as her hands flew to her hips and she glared defiantly at him.

"Well and you shall care, my girl. We are both bound by the terms of my uncle's will. We may not like one another, but I am at present acting as your guardian and shall discharge my duty which at present is to see you through a London Season and respectably wed!" The earl was seething as his own hot temper had been charged.

"*You,*" breathed Kitty as her hand moved to forestall her nanny who was mumbling something at her back, "are *not* my guardian."

"Am I not? Well then, we shall pay Mr. Harkins a visit tomorrow morning so that the facts may be plainly set forth for you. For the present, I suggest we drop the subject as I see Withers there, no doubt with the intelligence that our dinner awaits us!" So saying, the earl set down his glass of brandy and politely put out his arm for Kitty's hand. Kitty, however, snubbed him and with her head high, stomped out of the room before him.

The earl clenched his teeth and turned to Miss Diddles who whispered an apology, "Dear Kit does not yet understand. She is such a headstrong girl, spoiled and greatly encouraged by your dear uncle you see."

He patted Nanny's hand. "Never mind, Miss Diddles. It is of no consequence." This, oddly enough, was untrue. He found the little chit's snub irritating beyond understanding. She was nought but a country minx. Aye, he thought, a country minx who wanted taming and a great deal of training. Damnation. he was just the man who could manage the thing, just the one. Then nearly in the same thought, he did an about face; hell and fire, what was wrong with him? He would hand her over to his grandmother as fast he possibly could and wash his hands of the entire affair!

Eight

Henrietta sat alone in her mother's brightly papered morning room contentedly sipping her coffee. She had been reading a volume of Lord Byron's work and pensively wondering about the poet whom she had seen during her last London Season. Her thoughts were a maze of many when they exploded with the onslaught of a small whirlwind as Kitty rushed in upon her to exclaim in robust accents, "Ooooh, I tell you this, Ree, the earl has turned out to be the *most* insufferable man, so much worse than I feared. I told you how it would be, and you said I was just being fanciful. Well . . . he has been at Warton only one night, one night. and I am itching, just itching to land him a facer!"

"Kit!" laughed her friend. "You must learn to curb your tongue. Mama would have been greatly shocked to hear such language from you." Henrietta smiled as she put down the leather bound volume.

Kitty stopped and looked about. "But she isn't here."

"True, but you didn't know that when you came rushing in here, did you?" Henrietta Harkins was a good three years older than Kit and had always had a calming affect on Kitty's headiness. "However, I must be thankful that you at least are wearing some, er, sort of riding habit. Kit, you really must allow me to do something about your clothes."

"Well, and I am sorry," offered Kitty as she removed her hat and set it down on the nearby coffee table. "Riding side saddle is always such a task."

"And not beyond your skill!" retorted Henrietta scoffingly.

Kitty sighed as she regarded her old navy riding habit. It was well worn and quite out-dated. Indeed, it was a wonder it even fit her anymore. She pulled a face and eyed Henrietta, noting that her tall trim friend was looking very well indeed and was moved to concede, "Yes, you do have an eye, there is no gainsaying it and I really should let you teach me the knack of dressing." Kitty's eyes again scanned her friend with quiet consideration. "I tell you what, that gown suits you, Ree. It is a remarkably pretty shade of green and its cut is very elegant on your tall, light frame. Indeed, 'tis most becoming, and I suppose at my age, I should pay more attention to such things." However, Kit quickly dispensed with this and recalled her ruffled feelings, wagged a finger at the absent Earl of Halloway to say, "Still, he had no right."

It was certainly true that Henrietta's lack of beauty was made up by her sense of fashion and the manner in which she could carry herself when amongst friends. She smiled now and reached to grab Kitty's mobile finger and laughingly demand, "Whatever are you talking about? From the beginning, if you please?"

"There is nought to explain. It is self-evident. He is rude, he is conceited, he thinks me a country dowd—"

Henrietta giggled as she waved her hand over Kitty's appearance and made a sound. "Ahem."

Kitty stopped to pull a face and return a giggle. "Yes, well, but, so I am, one does not point out a person's blindness when he comes across someone who can not see?"

"Kit, of course not, but one can not alter a blind person's condition. Constructive criticism should be accepted in the light it is given, don't you think?"

"Yes . . . no . . . it's not the same, his criticism was given in a dark light. He was rude and arrogant."

"Well, it is certain he was not very wise," mused Henrietta.

"That is not all, Ree!" seethed Kit still fuming.

"My word, there is more? The earl certainly has been busy."

"He says he is my guardian and will be so until I marry!"

"Hmmmm? Well, you are only eighteen. I suppose someone must be your guardian?"

"Ree!" pronounced Kitty in accents that clearly indicated such words were a show of betrayal, "I am eighteen years old, after all, and no longer need a guardian. I consider myself quite self-sufficient. I won't have the earl as my guardian." She frowned over the problem. "Besides, your father never said a word about the earl being appointed my guardian."

"Well then, go in and see Papa at his office," suggested Henrietta reasonably.

"Indeed, I am supposed to accompany the earl at noon, we were to ride together . . ." Kitty made a most unladylike face and then stopped as a sudden thought came to mind. A sure light glistened in Kitty's china blue eyes. "Ree, I have just had a famous notion!"

"What?" returned Ree warily.

"I shall send a note telling the earl that I will meet him at your papa's office. In the meantime, Ree, you and I must go to town at once!"

"Kitty, what are you going to do?"

"Get a little self confidence, Ree, for the inevitable ride home with the illustrious Earl of Halloway."

Clayton Bickwerth counted the mound of bills in his hands and grinned broadly, well pleased with himself. Luckily he had managed to discover when Smilin' Jack would be taking his practice bout. Quietly he had watched him from a hole in the tent just one night ago as he went through his moves with his man. It was easy to see that the newcomer had speed and youth on his side. High odds were being given on the excited crowd's older favorite, Big Tom Brody. However, having had the opportunity to watch the strong newcomer in skilled action, Clayton placed a hefty sum against Big Tom in favor of the Smilin' Jack. The boxing match had been touted all over the county and there had been a large and eager betting crowd. Indeed, when the match was at end, Clayton found himself with a tidy sum!

"Well done!" said Harry jovially coming up behind him to give his shoulder a friendly push. "I had my money on Big Tom, but if ever there was a good match, t'was this one!" He eyed Clayton speculatively. "Come on, I'll buy you a tanker of ale over at the Bull and you will tell me what you saw in Smilin' Jack that *I* missed."

Clayton had other plans. There was no time to lose if he was going to court Miss Henrietta Harkins (and he couldn't hold off his creditors forever). She was an heiress, and he was not the only man in need of a convenient marriage. Thus, he smiled amiably and made a regretful click of his tongue.

"Can't. Sorry, Harry. Another time."

"Can't? Well, well." Harry grinned curiously, and then as he spotted Kitty and Henrietta coming out of Mrs. Sarah's Dress Shop, "By Jove! Will you look at Kit. Dressed to the nines!"

Kitty had just spent two hours as Henrietta and Mrs. Sarah worked to hem a lovely riding ensemble of royal blue with black frogging. Its fit was excellent, but it hung a few inches too long on her petite frame. Henrietta had brushed and set Kitty's hair in glorious gold ringlets at the back of her head and placed a matching royal blue top hat with a black veil on Kitty's fine head. White lace ruffles at her throat and wrist completed the elegant ensemble.

Kitty had stared at herself in disbelief, amazed that clothes could make such a difference, and when she and Ree stepped out, arm in arm, they were both jesting and laughing happily, well pleased with one another. They made a fetching picture.

"Kit? Zounds, man. Is that Kit?" ejaculated Clayton, half in earnest for he had never seen her in anything more feminine than a simple country gown.

"Aye, and Henrietta." Harry ran an appreciative eye over Ree, whom he had only really gotten to know in the last year, "Damn, but don't they *both* look stunning?"

Clayton eyed Henrietta whom he meant to have as wife and frowned. Certainly, her neatly fitting riding habit of light blue with dark blue trim was becoming, and her tall, trim figure quite attractive. But, stunning? No, he did not think so. Kitty, however had always caught his eye, even in her rags. He breathed his words, without deep thought, "Kitty is a beauty, there is no denying that. Miss Harkins . . . stunning?" He shook his head. "I would say rather, she has style, much more than personality and countenance."

Harry frowned at him, but allowed this to drop as he waved and went forward to meet the two young ladies. Clayton hurried along beside him, a far more intense purpose than his words could have supposed one to believe.

"Ho there, girl! The Warton hoyden, Kitty Kingsley, is it not?" Harry grinned jovially as he approached. He dodged Kit's gloved hand and beamed at Henrietta. "No doubt, we have *you* to thank for her metamorphosis?"

"And why do you suppose that?" laughed Henrietta.

"Why, Miss Harkins, the touch of your good taste, your style, your sheer elegance is handsomely writ all over Miss Kingsley's appearance!"

"That is a very fine, and a deserving compliment for Ree, but I take leave to tell you, Harry, that though I *think* somewhere in those words, there was a small compliment for me, it is so obscured that I rather think you should tread much more carefully from here on," warned Kit playfully as her kid gloved hands went to her well shaped hips. However, her attention suddenly slipped away as her deep blue eyes focused on a rider on a handsome snowy, grey gelding. The horse was prancing, restless and frightened of new sounds and things. The man's hands were quiet as he brought the spirited animal under him and managed him down the wide sandy road into the heart of town. To herself, and without consciously realizing it, Kitty acknowledged the Earl of Halloway's skill.

Harry brought her attention back to the fold as he laughed and took his chances. "Well then, I see you are reconciled, Kitty girl, and mean to take on the Beau Monde in fine fettle, eh? I thought you would come about after your meeting with the Earl of Halloway."

"Fie Harry, I rather thought *you* knew me better! If I choose to take on the ton, it will be for sport. What has the earl to do with me?"

Harry laughed. "Oh, take a damper! I only meant that perhaps the old gent talked you into behaving yourself."

"Behaving myself, behaving myself? Harry you . . . you big miserable dolt!" Kitty hissed as she lunged for his throat. She was really only half in earnest for even as he dodged her once more, she was smiling.

Ree screeched in horrified accents, "Kit! You wretched girl, remember where we are."

Clayton chuckled. "Oh do let her have at him. I think she will show to advantage."

Kit gave them a rueful smile. "Lucky for the heir of Brentwood that I must adhere to the proprieties." She eyed Harry thoughtfully and added quietly, "And the earl isn't old. At least not *that* old."

"Is he not?" asked Clayton in surprised accents. "I had a notion he must be at least fifty, if he is acting as your guardian . . ?"

"Well he is not even near fifty," scoffed Kitty and then added irritably, "and he is *not* my guardian." So saying she nodded toward Henrietta to sweetly smile. "As Henrietta's father shall soon point out to him." She touched Ree's shoulder, "Thank you, Ree for all your help."

Kitty then turned towards Clayton and the heir of Brentwood, put her chin well up and regally dismissed them with a polite, "Gentlemen."

Harry grinned as he called after her, "Well done, Miss Kingsley."

Kitty's newfound society manners vanished as she turned to stick her tongue out at him before dashing round the corner!

Nine

The earl had been met by a clerk upon his arrival at Mr. Harkins' office. As the lad went down the narrow hall to advise the solicitor of the earl's presence, he moved to the far wall and began a casual inspection of a wall map depicting the town and its surrounds.

The front door opened and as though a fresh zephyr had rushed him, he found Kitty bouncing into the room. The earl's hazel eyes snapped into focus and he could not help but note that she was looking splendid in her royal blue riding ensemble. He smiled to greet her. "Do my eyes deceive? I must say, Miss Kingsley, you astound me."

Astound him? What, did he think her some nothing country bumpkin with no style? Despite the fact, that she readily would have admitted this two days before, it irritated her now. "I am gratified," said Kitty with great aplomb, again always at her best when her temper had been ignited. She had wanted to display to the haughty earl that she could flaunt style and fashion with the best of them. However, his compliment came through a backdoor and she was all too aware of this.

"Indeed. I fully expected you to arrive in

breeches and a peaked cap!" he shot back at her annoyed by her set down. The little chit certainly had a sharp tongue, he thought with a brooding look, but even through his irritation he could not help but notice the deep blue brilliance of her large warm eyes.

"Really?" returned Miss Kingsley giving him a cold smile as she went before him down the hall toward Mr. Harkins' office. "I can't imagine why you would think that?"

"Because, Miss Kingsley I have been privileged to see you in in your heathen uniform and have been plainly advised it is your favorite mode of dress on and off Warton grounds!" he snapped, now completely ready to administer a spanking, should his newly adopted position of guardian to the wayward chit allow.

Kitty's blue eyes flashed, but she decided to confound him by turning him up sweet. She was without town polish but with an abundance of instincts. "Indeed, I was persuaded that would not have pleased you, my lord."

"And pleasing *me*, was of course your first priority?" The earl requested caustically.

"Should it not be?" Kitty's cherry lips parted deliciously. He found her full lips pursed as they were, provocatively desirable. He brushed this thought aside, and decided to take her lead. Composing himself, he replied quietly, "Though, my dear, I doubt that it is, I would hope that it were so, at least while you are in my charge." There, he thought, he had scored a hit.

His words distressed her. She could not be,

would not be in his charge. It was unthinkable. She would not allow him to take control of her life! However, even as she felt herself start to frenzy, she pulled on her good sense. Dash it! She would not allow his ill chosen words to alter her outward air of calm. She knew better than that, and besides she told herself confidently, Mr. Harkins would straighten him out. She gave him a saucy look and though her blue eyes still glinted with suppressed anger, she quietly said, "If you please, my lord, you must understand that I am eighteen and completely capable of taking charge of my own life. You are under a misapprehension if you believe that I am in your charge. *I am not.* If I chose to please you by dressing the part you expect me to perform in public, 'tis simply that I wished my nanny might not come under your censure."

"Be clear on one thing. I would not dream of censuring Miss Diddles for any of *your* foibles." He took a breath and steadied himself. This one wanted manners and training, and he was just the one to manage the feat. "As to the rest, my dear Miss Kingsley, it just so happens that I had a letter from my uncle, and he did *not* think an eighteen year old female fully capable of taking charge of her life. Instead, he entrusted your future and well being to me." Halloway eyed her loftily believing he had won the round. "You are mistaken if you think otherwise."

The door before them opened then to display Mr. Harkins within its wide frame. He looked from one to the other before ushering them inside with a brisk greeting. This was certainly a very strained situation. Harkins took a moment to eye both the earl and Kitty over his spectacles. They stood before him, very nearly glaring at one another. Pity, he thought with an inward sigh. He cleared his throat to catch their attention and softly suggested, "Please, won't you both be seated?" Zounds! He could feel the tension ripple in the air. He decided the best course would be to ignore it.

Kitty gingerly took her place on the leather chair Mr. Harkins had pulled out for her and avoided the earl's sharp hazel eyes. How they had glittered green and amber as he had regarded her! How tall and handsome . . . no, insufferably proud and arrogant he was. Their situation was absurd. So horribly absurd!

"The note your messenger delivered to my home early this morning was very clear. However, I regret to say, the answer to the question at hand is not clear at all, and leaves us with something of a problem." Mr. Harkins started to say as he looked from Kitty to the Earl of Halloway.

"I don't see that, Mr. Harkins. I have agreed to go to London, but, do please advise the earl that he is *not* my guardian. I am, after all, eighteen." Kitty cut in quickly but managed a sweet smile all the same. She had no very clear idea where Henrietta's father's sympathies lay. She had often spent wonderful times at Ree's home, but, whenever she had encountered Mr. Harkins there he had been busy at his desk or on his way out. He had always seemed a distant sort of man, though

Ree obviously adored him. She watched him speculatively now and felt seriously uneasy by his reaction to her words.

"It was my understanding that Miss Kingsley's future welfare had been entrusted to my keeping," stuck in the earl quick to make his point. "In fact . . ." Halloway reached into the folds of his buff suede riding coat and produced a folded letter, "My uncle specifically requested this of me."

Mr. Harkins took up the letter and hastily perused it. "Yes, I am fully cognizant of your uncle's dying wishes. In spite of that, we have a dilemma."

"Why should this be a dilemma?" demanded Kitty going forward on her chair.

"Because my dear, this letter certainly does in fact request the Earl of Halloway to undertake your care, well being and initiate a situation in which you would be in a position to find an eligible match. It is a specific stipulation of the conditions of Edwin Warton's will. There can be no mistaking his intentions."

"Aha!" The earl's hazel eyes glinted as he regarded Miss Kingsley.

Mr. Harkins put up his hand to forestall Kitty's agitation, "However, legally, and this is the trick of it, Warton did not *legally* appoint the earl or anyone else as your guardian when he drew up his new will."

"Ha!" called Kitty, "So be it!"

Again, Harkins' hand went up. "Still . . . we can not ignore the fact that Warton, in his new will requests you, Kitty, to enjoy a London Season, or

Seasons, whichever the case may be, under the excellent auspices of his nephew, the Earl of Halloway. You can not very well do that without being, so to speak, in his charge and under his protection. Now there it is, my girl."

"This is insufferable. I won't have it," objected Kitty getting to her feet.

"You needn't of course, adhere to your guardian's dying wish." Mr. Harkins said quietly.

Kitty sat down again and her lashes brushed her flushed cheeks, *"That,* I must do."

"Then, if I may make a suggestion?" Clearly they needed, thought Harkins, an arbitrator, "Make the best of an uncomfortable situation. Call a truce."

"He is not my guardian. I will not take orders from him as though I were a mere child," Kitty retorted stubbornly.

Mr. Harkins had another avenue to travel. Quickly, before the earl could fire angry words at Kitty, he managed to catch his attention, "My lord, may I assume that you will be escorting Kitty to London in the very near future?"

The earl inclined his head. "Certainly, whether she will it or not." He glared in her direction.

She ruffled up and would have retorted had not Harkins immediately said, "But, I understood yours were bachelor lodgings in London."

"I had my grandmother go before me to my house in Kensington Square. She is preparing for our arrival and will be my hostess (if Miss Kingsley's manners do not put her off) during the Season." He raised his eyes heavenward and made a quiet, but audible plea, "May there be only one . . ."

He was of course inciting the volatile creature to riot. He knew it, but then he had been goaded. Mr. Harkins did not approve and cleared his throat. "Ahem. Well, then, Miss Kingsley will be a guest in your house and be in the enviable position of having the Countess of Halloway to give her guidance as she enters society. I have met her on one occasion, and found her an estimable woman." He turned to Kitty, "As a guest of the earl's, in the earl's house, you will agree that custom dictates that you behave within the boundaries of his wishes. I trust this is acceptable to you?"

Reluctantly, Kitty acceded. "Yes."

"Fine. There is your truce." He gave Kitty a considering look. "And Kitty, need I remind you that the earl is now master of Warton Castle and all its holdings?"

"I understand that . . . but . . ." Kitty's eyes had narrowed as she anticipated the rest.

"Do you, my dear?" Harkins continued, "I hope so." He looked away from her to the earl. "As I have just reminded Kitty, it is true that you own the Castle and all its holdings, however, Edwin Warton's principal fortune will continue to be held in trust for you until you have fulfilled the terms of the will. You may of course draw on the interest in the interim."

A moment of silence followed his little speech. He wasn't quite sure what more was expected of him. He had been very fond of Edwin Warton and though he had never approved of the manner in which Warton allowed young Kitty to roam the countryside, he knew that she was a dear friend of his Henrietta. He did not like to see her so obviously overcome by agitation. However, she would soon be enjoying London's Beau Monde and all they had to offer. Thus, mentally relieving himself of all wayward concerns, he made them both one last offer, "Well then have either of you any further questions?"

The earl and Kitty finally agreed on something. Neither one could think what more they could ask. Both wished they were not trapped in the situation in which they found themselves, but they could see Harkins could do nought to spare them this.

Harkins got to his feet and extended his hand to the earl, "Then I believe this concludes our meeting. Godspeed." To Kitty he again regarded her over his spectacles. "Enjoy yourself, young lady. That was what your guardian wanted above all else."

"Yes, sir. Thank you, sir." Kitty smiled. But she wondered however could she enjoy herself with the earl taking over her life.

Ten

A breeze had picked up and the sunny April morning had turned decidedly cool. The earl was irritably aware that the weather was not the only thing freezing him. This was a new experience for him. He was an extraordinarily handsome gentleman, with a respected title and cavalier charm. He had until recently been favored by women's preference for his magnetic company. In the last year, he had received a sure jolt when he had watched Shawna's youthful infatuation for him dissolve. He had been further startled to find that Shawna actually preferred his far more sedate cousin, Roland. At first, the knowledge had completely astounded him out of his habitual conceit. However, he quickly put his disconcertion to rest. He peacefully explained it to himself. After all, he had not bent to his grandmother's will and obeyed her dictum and proposed to her beloved ward, Shawna. He had not even made the smallest attempt to really court Shawna, thinking she would be there for the taking when he was good and ready. Thus, he told himself, she had turned to Roland. He had shrugged this off for although he had been keenly fond of Shawna he had never been in love with her.

Love? An irregular emotion that he was heartily glad he was completely and totally immune to. He had never been in love. Infatuated, charmed, enchanted, yes, but love? Never. This was an immunity he cherished. Judging by what he had observed, this was not a comfortable position for a man to find himself in. Time had certainly spared him, and after all his experience with a variety of beautiful and captivating women, he was pleased to find himself still free. He was seven-and-twenty and had known many exquisite, sophisticated, genuinely desirable women in every sense, and not once had he felt himself wanting more than to take them to bed. In that effort he had been extremely successful as his tastes never extended toward the innocent. That was a rule never to be broken. He did not play hard and fast with the uninitiated. Thus, he had very little knowledge about women of Kitty's age and no experience whatsoever with anyone of Kitty's stamp! She was an enigma to him.

As they rode in silence out of the now bustling town, he tried to make polite conversation. Just what did one talk about with a rustic child? He looked her over and remarked, "We must see about getting you a sidesaddle before we leave for London, so that you may learn its use. Your riding ensembles will take less stress and better show to advantage when properly draped over your horse." He meant no offense. He had simply noticed that she was riding astride and that the skirt of her new riding habit was bunching up and becoming wrinkled.

Kitty felt herself bristle but restrained her sharp tongue, saying only, "Oh, but I *have* a side saddle. It was given to me by Uncle Edwin and I learned the skill many years ago, my lord. My preference is to ride astride."

"That may be, but you can not ride astride in Hyde Park. It isn't done, my girl." He heard himself, and felt a fool. What was he doing, extolling the proprieties? The role did not suit him. Indeed, he had always taken a wild joy in breaking any number of society's strictest rules.

She felt herself start to hiss, but got control. She would show him she could handle society manners! "Of course, it isn't. I quite understand. However, as you can see, I am not yet in London, and this," she waved her gloved hand, "is not Hyde Park."

Inwardly he heard himself say, touche, for he was fair enough minded to know that he deserved that. He had done nothing but ride the chit since he had arrived. Some of this showed in his bright hazel eyes which suddenly twinkled at her as he inclined his head, "Right you are Miss Kingsley! This is certainly not Hyde Park, and I know *I* am sporting for a run."

She eyed him dubiously for a moment before smiling to answer, "Done!"

In the meantime, Henrietta found herself flanked on her ride home by both Harry and Clayton. While Clay found his friend, Harry's company a hindrance to his romancing, Ree was supremely glad of it. She was comforted by Harry's familiar and light conversation. He had a way of always putting her at her ease and at her best.

Clayton's sudden attentions were making her painfully shy. However with Harry present she was able to maintain an easy banter without slipping into stammering half-sentences.

Harry laughed over Ree's description of Kitty's antics while she had been fitted for her new riding habit and shook his head to say, "You are a wonder, Henrietta. I don't know how you made her stand still."

She smiled. "Oh, she isn't so very difficult. It is just that she doesn't like strangers ordering her about, and though this Earl of Halloway is the heir of Warton, he is a stranger to poor Kitty."

"Aye . . . poor Kitty indeed!" agreed Clay forcefully. "The way I hear it, the earl was a stranger to Warton as well. It isn't fair that she should lose all."

Henrietta rushed to answer. "Oh, no, I am sure . . ." She thought better of repeating matters she was certain must be confidential and stammered something inaudible.

Harry hurriedly intervened. "Oh well as to that, Clay, you must not think Kit was left penniless. I understand she has quite a respectable dowry and a most comfortable competence. In addition to that, her entire Season is being funded by the terms of Warton's will."

"Is that right?" mused Clayton. "Well still, it isn't quite what she was due."

"Oh, please," objected Henrietta, "we should not be discussing Kitty's affairs like this."

Harry immediately added his voice. "Quite right, Henrietta, no doubt Kit would have our heads!"

Clayton laughed this off though his mind was busily working. Could he be happy on an easy competence? He would have Kit for wife, but only enough money to live his days out as a country squire. That was not what he wanted. No. He needed to put his estates in order. He needed to go to London, set up a house there, join White's, gamble, buy flash horses . . . He needed more, much more than an easy competence. He sighed sadly over this because the more time he spent with Henrietta Harkins the less he wanted her for wife. However, as they reached the end of her front drive he was quick to jump from his horse and help her dismount. With her waist still in his gloved hands, he looked long into her light brown eyes and softly said, "Thank you, Miss Harkins."

She nervously laughed, "For what, Mr. Bickwerth?"

"For the treasured joy of your company. May I call on you tomorrow morning?"

She flushed with pleasure. "I would like that."

Harry watched them with a growing frown and when she was indoors and he and Clay were urging their horses back toward the pike he roundly inquired, "Now, *what* was *that* about?"

"Am I stepping on your toes, dearest Harry?" laughed Clay not at all disconcerted.

Harry was irritated. "No, dammit, but since when did you start having an interest in that direction, my buck?"

"You weren't listening, Harry. I only said I did not find her . . . stunning," Clay responded glibly.

"Well, this sudden interest in Henrietta amazes me. When did your tastes move in that particular direction?" It was odd, but he found himself very perturbed to discover Clay was contemplating courting Miss Hawkins. He certainly wasn't the man for Kitty and he was heartily glad *that* apparently was at an end, but no more was he the man for Henrietta. Society would of course, smile at such a match. Still, Henrietta was not the sort for a marriage of convenience. She was far too sensitive and caring to lead such a coldly calculating life.

"Only recently," Clay lightly responded. What difference his interest in Miss Harkins could mean to Harry was beyond his understanding. No doubt, Harry was just curious.

"You mean don't you, only after you found out Kit wasn't to inherit a fortune!" accused Harry right on the mark.

"Harold, you have overstepped." said Clay with a sudden angry light in his pale blue eyes.

"Oh go take a damper!" retorted Harry picking up the pace.

Clay laughed suddenly and said, "What we need, dear Harry is a run. Are you game?"

"Am I game?" repeated Harry getting into position, "To the next milepost then!"

Kitty was the first to bring in her horse as they reached the crossroads. She could see Clay and Harry galloping at them in a steady cloud of dust. She laughed and raised a hand, at the same time steadying her horse under her for her mare pranced and fidgeted all too excitedly at the arrival of new horses.

The earl too, was bringing his big grey under him as the gelding danced in place. His voice soothed, "Ho there, lad, ho." He sat his horse well and there was no doubt whatsoever to any onlooker that though the young gelding was spirited, the earl could keep him in control.

"Oh, he *is* handsome!" Kitty declared as she watched the earl work him in place. The young gelding was arching his wide white neck and snorting nervously as the two new horses and their riders slowed to an approaching walk.

Kitty quickly made the necessary introductions before moving her horse into position beside Harry. Their horses were long time friends and fell into a comfortable pace, leaving Clay and the earl to bring up the rear.

"Well then, m'girl," inquired Harry. "How did your meeting go? All settled, right and tight?"

"Hardly," grimaced Kitty, "Mr. Harkins calls it a dilemma. He says that the earl is not legally my guardian, yet, he is required to address such a position because of the terms of the will. Terms, both the earl and I find ourselves trapped by."

"What precisely does that mean?"

"Indeed, you may well ask." Kitty sighed. "The long and the short of it, Harry, is that we have opted for something of a truce. Mr. Harkins played arbitrator and I felt a mere child. He drew a picture for me, you see. I shall be a guest in the earl's household, under the Countess of Halloway's guidance and must, therefore do the polite. The earl will be my host and Mr. Harkins has adjured him not ride roughshod over me."

"Egad, Kit I can well imagine how you must have felt." Harry responded and then after a moment's consideration. "But, you know, I think you will do. He seems a charming sort of chap, though m'father says the situation is bizarre."

"Bizarre is a very good word for it." mused Kitty. "But, Harry, why does your father say that?"

"Well, apparently he knows *of* the earl, and says he is too young and too much a rogue to take on the care of a gently bred young woman, especially you."

"Rogue? That was what I thought before he came here. I tell you what Harry, I don't think so any longer. Why, he is forever preaching the proprieties to me. Rogue indeed!" And then as another thought fluttered in her busy brain. "What did your father mean, especially me?"

Trapped, Harry laughed. "Well, Kit, you ain't quite the normal young maid, now are you?"

As an answer, Kitty hauled off and rapped his

arm, though she giggled happily, secretly well pleased with this dictum.

At their backs, the earl watched them with keen interest. Here now was a possible romance? Could it be? Right under his nose, a suitor to save him the long Season? An avenue to be pursued?

Eleven

Late afternoon found Kitty out of her new ensemble and once more defiantly clothed in her tight moulded and supremely comfortably aged breeches. Her old suede short coat kept the chill off her back as she sat along the edge of the wide rushing rocky stream that passed through Warton Park and soothed her frenzied nerves. She had cast her fishing line, though truth to tell she wasn't at all concentrating on the art. Her mind was full of the evils that lay ahead of her.

There would be no more peaceful fishing, no more wildly galloping about the countryside she so loved. There would be no more breeches. There would be no more sitting comfortably with cook in the nether regions of the kitchen and munching on treats straight out of the oven. There would be instead, the earl, his grandmother and the miserable constraint of endless rules . . . Faith, it was horrible to contemplate, even in the abstract.

A sound brought her head up and around to find a tall lithe young woman walking towards her and she blinked. "Ree, what a wonderful surprise. Whatever brings you here at this time of day?" It occurred to Kitty that her friend was looking quite blushingly radiant. "Here sit beside me, its dry."

"Kitty, we need to talk," Henrietta said as she dropped down beside her friend.

"Don't we just," sighed Kitty.

"After you left me today to go for your meeting with my father, both Harry and Clayton Bickwerth were kind enough to escort me home." Henrietta lowered her lashes.

"Ha!" laughed Kitty with a shake of her head, "There I was under fire and there you were . . . hmmm . . . er, just *what* were you doing, Ree my girl?"

Henrietta smiled happily. "Kit, you wretched child. It was quite gratifying and just a bit awkward, you know I have never been flanked by such handsome gentlemen before . . ."

Kitty eyed her for a long moment and then as sudden dawning lit in her active brain she laughed. "Oh, Ree, my poor dear, two bucks at once. However did my shy miss manage that?"

"Well as to that, it wasn't so very difficult because one of those bucks as you call them, was Harry."

"I've always suspected Harry had an eye in your direction, but, no, you would never hear of it," mused Kitty much entertained by her friend's discomfiture.

"Nonsense, that is not so at all, Kitty, I know you will say again that Harry is forever tagging along when you and I are together, but that is because of you, not me." She shook her head,

"You will never credit it, I know *I* should not, yet, it is Mr. Bickwerth who has well . . . he has . . ."

"Has what, you silly girl? I would never credit what?"

"I think he . . . has a decided preference in my regard. I can't believe it . . . but, well— "

"Devil a bit!" ejaculated Kitty cutting her off, and then deplorably honest, adding, "And you are right, I can hardly credit it. What in heaven's name did he do to make you think so?"

"Kit, you really must learn to curb those cant expressions. It won't do." Henrietta who never failed to find herself shocked by her outspoken friend, and not at all insulted by Kitty's open disbelief, laughed. She too, still found it impossible to believe that Clay meant to pay her court.

"Never mind that," breathed Kitty excitedly. "Tell me what has happened."

Henrietta turned a bright shade of crimson and did not meet Kitty's probing blue eyes, "Clayton asked if he could call on me tomorrow. And he was most particular in his attentions on our ride home, and Kitty, when he helped me off my horse, he held my waist . . ." she sighed happily, "just so . . ." It was obvious that she had been flattered by the attention.

"Just so, eh?" Kitty laughed ruefully. She was taken aback and needed a moment to consider this new development. This new and startling information about Clayton Bickwerth did *not* jibe with her acute instincts. Henrietta was not precisely the sort of woman to arouse Clay to desire. In fact, she was more than a little surprised that he had already turned on his charm for someone else. Until very recently Kitty had been aware of his very pronounced courtship in her regard. There was no denying that, like Harry, she was mildly fond of Clay. She enjoyed his habitual air of good humor, his sense of fun and the fact that he was a lively and charming companion. However, she knew that she was in no danger of losing her heart to him. Henrietta on the other hand, was most vulnerable at this time in her life. She was one-and-twenty and had suffered two unsuccessful Seasons. Staid and practical, Henrietta was starved for romance and if she fell for the likes of Clayton Bickwerth, she would fall hard. Kitty frowned over this because she couldn't wouldn't allow her friend to be hurt. There too, Kitty found herself even a little shocked to discover her usually clear minded, sensible friend so completely impressed with the rakish fellow.

"Ree, do you want him to pay you court?" Kitty inquired slowly.

Henrietta was honest above all else. She flung up her hands and then rested them beneath her chin which she set on the knees she had pulled up under her heavy riding skirt, "Yes, no. It is just that I never really had a beau show any real interest in me when I was in London, except for Waldo Brooks and Waldo, though a very decent and pleasant man was nearly forty, bald, and wore spectacles like Papa's." She looked away for a moment. "It just felt so very nice to be the object of such a sophisticated young man's attention, and Kitty, he is so very very handsome . . ."

"Hmmmm, he is that. Much like an Adonis. However, I don't think he is the sort of man for you, Ree."

This irritated Henrietta and she frowned. "Why, because I am too plain for him?"

"Idiot. You know better. Oh Ree, I have always thought you were pretty, no, *more* than pretty. You have style, grace, elegance. You have heart and a pure sweet aura."

"But— ? There is a *but* in there?" Ree sighed outloud as she took Kitty's free hand. "You may be open with me, Kitty, I want you to please tell me . . . what is the but?"

"You want me to be open? Right then my girl, and I shall make no bones about it. Clay may look like an Adonis, but he has the heart of a cad. There, I have said it. It's my opinion and I *could* be wrong . . ."

"Yes, you could be, you know," Ree said earnestly. She desperately wanted Kitty to be wrong. She returned her hands to her knees and after rocking a moment offered, "You see, Kit . . . it was ever so nice having this wildly charming cavalier make up to me."

Kitty laughed. "So be it. Enjoy yourself, but hide your heart from him, my girl." She suddenly stopped as a notion struck her. "Ree, what you need is another Season in London."

"*No!* I do not." Henrietta retorted animately. "Whatever put such a nonsensical notion into that zany brain of yours?" She shook her head. "I won't put myself through that again, besides, Mama can't manage it this year."

"Not with your Mama, *with me!*" exclaimed Kitty.

"Oh, no. I couldn't. And don't you think you should ask permission of the earl before you go inviting guests to his house?" Henrietta giggled. "A mad woman, that is what I am truly convinced you are."

"So I am, but think of the fun we could have. Oh Ree, you must. It will be perfect." Kitty sighed. "If he weren't so arrogant, conceited and self-serving, I might have better tolerated him."

"You still can't invite me without his permission . . ," insisted Henrietta.

"Absurd girl, the earl won't forbid me a house guest. He may be many things, but he isn't an ogre after all."

"How very pleased I am to hear it," said an all too familiar voice at their backs.

Both girls twisted round to find the earl hovering over them. It was Henrietta's first real look at the earl and she sat studying him while his hazel eyes twinkled appreciatively and Kitty blushed and glared all at once, "My lord . . . I did not hear you approach . . ."

"Obviously," he returned tongue in cheek.

She laughed all at once. "Well, it is a poor beginning, but do please allow me to make known to you my dear friend, Miss Henrietta Harkins . . . the Earl of Halloway."

The two exchanged a moment's polite amenity before Kitty eyed the earl curiously to inquire, "Out for an afternoon's stroll by the water, my lord?" It crossed her mind that he was mountainously tall, and ruggedly good-looking. As soon as the thought entered her mind she shrugged it off.

"Not exactly. I thought that you might like to know that I have made up an impromptu dinner for your entertainment this evening. I have invited your gentlemen friends, young Harry Brentwood and Clay Bickwerth." The earl eyed Henrietta. "I thought it might be pleasant for Miss Kingsley to have an evening with her friends before we depart for London. Please, Miss Harkins, forgive the lateness of the invitation, but I can see that you, too, are one of Miss Kingsley's intimates. I am certain a farewell dinner would be incomplete without your presence."

"Oh, I don't know."

"Yes, oh Ree, you must," said Kitty excitedly.

Henrietta agreed to it and Kitty immediately and impulsively turned to the earl. "How very thoughtful and kind of you, my lord. Thank you."

The earl had his own agenda. His actions had not been based on kindness but on expediency. It was his intention to encourage a romance between Harry and his termagant charge. At the very least it could serve as a back-up if she did not secure a husband in London. Her genuine gratitude shot a wave of guilt through him. She looked a veritable child, and it occurred to him that even in her breeches with her yellow hair a mass of curls to her waist, she was quite beautiful.

"Nonsense," he returned jovially. "As you pointed out to Miss Harkins, I am not an ogre."

"Oh!" Kitty exclaimed all at once and grabbed firm hold of her fishing rod. "I've got one!"

Twelve

Kitty's bedroom door opened wide and Henrietta glided within saying excitedly though unnecessarily, "I'm here."

Kitty looked round from her contemplation of herself in the long looking glass to laugh. "So you are. And, Ree, that shade of soft green does suit you!"

"Thank you. You look beautiful, Kit." Henrietta sighed wistfully. "Do you know how many girls would die to have your color hair?"

"No, and it wouldn't do them any good if they were dead." Kitty laughed. "But, Ree, I can't be seen in this." Her hands moved expressively over herself. "I look like a schoolgirl!" Kitty frowned at the reflection of herself in the mirror. "What can be done? I just never bothered about fashion before and now, I quite see that this just won't do!"

"Let me see," said Ree giving her another once over. "Do you know what? You don't need this." Henrietta tugged at the bow in the center of the curve of the gown's scoop neck. It didn't come off so she moved to Kitty's vanity and found a small pair of scissors and made a quick, clean snip. "There, that is so much better."

"Yes . . . I see . . ."

"And you don't need all this lace. It makes the neckline far higher than is fashionable. This upper tier can easily be eliminated," Ree offered after another moment's consideration. The removal of the lace flounce round the neckline took a moment longer, but when it was done, it was obvious that Kitty was not a schoolgirl.

"Oh, that is better!" Kitty exclaimed, well pleased with the new look. It was still a simple blue muslin evening gown, but its lines now displayed her own to advantage.

"Now, little girl, all this hair?" said Henrietta taking up a hair brush. "I take off the ribbon and pin it up at the top of your head." That done, Ree stood back and said, "Look and tell me what say you?"

"I say you are a genius!" ejaculated Kitty beaming happily.

"Am I? Perhaps you will explain why it is so important all of a sudden for you to look fashionable." Henrietta's brow was up quizzically.

"Because there is a demon in me that wants to show that pink of the ton downstairs, that I can be more than just a country bumpkin!"

"Why?" pursued Henrietta. "You never cared a fig for anyone's opinion's before."

"Not true, Ree I care about the opinions of people who matter to me."

"Does the Earl of Halloway matter to you?"

"Don't be absurd. It is just that, well, I suppose I feel challenged by him."

"How so?"

"He doesn't think me capable of managing the transition from country life into the world of the Beau Monde. He does not understand that I have chosen to be what I am, here at Warton, but that doesn't mean I can't be whatever it takes as the need arises."

"Ah, of course," Henrietta answered dubiously. It wasn't so very long ago that Kitty had claimed she could not cope amongst the sophisticated Beau Monde. If ever there was a completely contrary character, it was Kitty Kingsley.

At that moment, the Earl of Halloway found himself playing host in the library to both Harry and Clayton. They had already managed to imbibe a respectable quantity of brandy, and were much in spirits. They quickly discovered that horses, hounds and the chase, were common ground and lively conversation ensued. As anecdotes, and experiences were shared with great vivacity, the earl regarded his younger companions with something close to wonder. What had happened to him? He was only seven-and-twenty, only a few years older than these lads, and yet, for some inexplicable reason, he felt a century older. The years on the town had left him jaded. He could not help feeling as he watched Clay and Harry exchange friendly banter, much like an outsider. Harry burst into innocent laughter at that mo-

ment over some nonsense Clay had uttered and
the earl smiled. He liked Harry. He was a pleasant
lad with a good heart. If he had to choose a man,
between the two, he definitely preferred the heir
of Brentwood for his spitfire upstairs. Why it
should matter who Kitty chose, as long as the
choice was amongst their own class, was not a question he bothered to ask himself. He only knew
that there was something calculating in Clay that
did not appeal to him. However, that aside, there
was no denying that Clay was just the sort of young
blade to turn a simple maid's head.

As the earl contemplated the possibilities, the
library double doors quietly opened to display in
a splatter of pale blue and mint green, both Kitty
and Miss Harkins, their faces alive with ready
laughter. Henrietta's mood was light and easy
with Kit as a bolster beside her. The two girls exchanged amused looks as Kitty merrily bounced
into the cozy room, ready to sport with her friends.
All the while she couldn't shake the feeling that
the earl was watching her and inexplicably the notion made her tingle with excitement.

They had been immediately met by a loud show
of enthusiasm. Both Harry and Clay had joyfully
raised their glasses to them, as the earl had moved
to the sideboard to quietly, unobtrusively pour
each of the girls a glass of mild madeira.

Harry went on to heartily exclaim, "By Jupiter,
we are blessed gentlemen, are we not? I say, here
we have angels of beauty."

Henrietta received this with a soft smile and
downcast lashes, sweetly just as she ought. Kitty

laughed to say, "Pray, Harry, you are outrageous. What is all this jack-pudding flattery?"

"No, no, don't stop him," objected Henrietta as she moved towards young Brentwood and raised her eyes to his handsome face, "It is so *very* well done."

Harry smiled at her, noting that her eyes were a soft shade of brown, lit with gentleness. He felt a little flushed (no doubt from the brandy) but, found himself generously inspired by the same to new heights of dalliance, he returned in gallant tones, "Oh, but my dear Henrietta, it is truth . . . sweet truth."

Clay had found himself drawn toward Kitty, but his brows came together as he heard Harry's bold flirtation with Henrietta. He certainly didn't want Harry moving wildly in on his chosen target. After all, Harry had no need to hang out for a rich wife. Good sense reassured him. Harry was simply being kind. That was Harry. Surely, if Harry were ready to walk down the aisle, Kitty would be the one he would pursue. Thus, Clay set himself at ease and moved closer still to Kitty. Henrietta would only think he was making his farewells, and besides, if she became a trifle jealous, it would only serve to make his suit all the more desirable. The fact was, he simply could not get his intense gaze away from Kitty. She was ravishing. He had never seen her figure so advantageously displayed and she was smiling so very flirtatiously his way.

"You will take London by storm," Clay whispered softly.

"Will I?" laughed Kitty sweetly. She had

watched the earl give Henrietta a glass of madeira and move in her direction. As he handed her the delicately long stemmed crystal glass, she eyed him saucily. *"My lord* does *not* think so."

Clay looked up at the earl with genuine surprise. *"That,* I simply can not believe."

"Do tell him, my lord. Am I not right?" pursued Kitty.

"Tell him what, minx? I was not privy to the first part of your conversation?" The earl had heard every word, but he meant to teach her manners.

Kitty's instincts were on the alert. He would not be led onto dangerous ground. Whatever he thought, however he felt about her, he would not betray himself in company with abject rudeness. She discovered that she liked that in him. It was a gentleman's strict code of honor. This she had heard enough times from Harry. "Ethics and principles, at least," Harry would gravely add, "a *gentlemen's* ethics and principles, were things a gently bred female could never understand, governed, as females were, by emotions." Kitty had always wanted to kick him after just such a speech. Remembering this now, she was able to giggle sweetly before taking a sip of her wine. She also managed to give the earl a most naughty look as she did so, before saying, "We are saved, you and I, my lord, here is Nanny . . ." Kitty immediately took a few steps towards Miss Diddles as the elderly woman approached and immediately put an affectionate arm about her thin shoulders. "I was wondering where you could possibly be."

"Och, I was in the kitchen helping that poor lad of the earl's. He got kicked proper by one of the earl's carriage horses. Put a nice cooling poultice to his leg."

"Why thank you, Miss Diddles. Max is a good lad, and that was very kind of you," said the earl going towards her and giving her a slight bow.

"Indeed, Nanny, I don't know what any of us would ever do without you."

Nanny blushed happily and then with a sweetly shy smile, put her hands together to announce, "I am told that dinner awaits our pleasure."

"Then lead us to it, Nanny dear!" ejaculated Harry jovially as he bent an arm for Henrietta's hand.

The earl inclined his head and smiled as he offered Nanny his arm and then led the way, leaving Clay to escort Kitty and bring up the rear.

Thirteen

Miss Diddles slumped against the plump leather squabs of the coach. Kitty eyed her for a moment, before whispering, "Nanny? Are you asleep, Nanny?"

A short snort and a long wheezy snore was Kitty's answer and she smiled to herself as she angled the carriage pillow behind the elderly woman's neck. A moment later she turned her attention once more to the passing scenery. It was not even eight o'clock in the morning, and they had already been on the road for at least two hours. It was an odd thing for, she hadn't at all minded the early rising, but she had been most surprised when the earl had scheduled their dawn departure. Indolence, did not seem to be among the earl's many faults. Kitty had it strongly in her mind that the Earl of Halloway, surely, never left his bed before nine o'clock! Well, in that, she had been wrong.

She sighed as she recalled their small dinner party with her friends. How she would miss Harry. When the Harkins' carriage came to fetch Henrietta, she had clung to her and took a promise that she would at least try and visit her in London.

Everything was all so strange! What she needed now was a ride!

She had worn her riding habit. This was for the practical reason that she had not enough time to have a traveling ensemble made for the trip to London. Well, the earl's coach was well sprung and comfortable, but she had no intention of wasting the loveliness of the morning within its luxurious confines! Instinctively, she had not mentioned anything about wishing to ride, to the earl. Somehow, she knew what his answer would be. Now, all she needed was the opportunity.

She had not long to wait for this, as suddenly the coach began to slow to a halt as Max wielded the conveyance to the side of the road. Kitty hurriedly pinned her royal blue top hat in place and scrambled unceremoniously out the carriage door.

"Is everything all right, Max. Is your leg giving you trouble?" Kitty asked solicitously as Max, an apologetic smile on his youthful countenance limped towards her. "M'leg be fine. Miss Diddles did me right and tight last evenin', she did." He shook his head, "It be old Star, miss. Think 'ee is about to lose a shoe. Jest thought Oi'd 'ave a look-see."

"Fine," said Kitty brightly. "While you do that, I'll saddle my mare."

"Oi can do that fer ye, miss." he frowned over this new problem. The earl had said nought about Miss Kingsley taking to horse. What the earl had made infinitely clear was the fact that he was to keep a sharp eye, and make certain all went

smoothly. Max took this order to infer that his job
was to protect the female occupants of the earl's
coach from the ever-present dangers of highway-
men. This was not something he felt was a realistic
threat in broad daylight on this particular main
road. Still, one never knew about the bridle culls
and so, he had in fact kept an eye over his shoulder. This, however, was out of his realm! How was
he to protect Miss Kingsley if she meant to take
to horse unescorted on the Post Road? After all,
there were other threats to a young beautiful and
unprotected female on the open road. It was heavily traveled by sporting gentlemen for one. Oh,
no no, Max was sure the earl would not approve
of this at all and was moved to protest, "The thing
is, miss, O've a strong notion, ye see, that his lordship will 'ave me 'ead fer this. He left me to taike
care of ye and Miss Diddles, ye see. Oi can't do
that, can Oi, if ye go off all alone." Max shook his
head. "The earl won't loike it."

Kitty's blue eyes glinted defiantly. "Would he
not?"

Max quickly stuck in, for he could see he had
said something that had angered her. "Aye then,
and it will be bellows to mend fer the thing is 'ee
would be in the right of it, now, miss. Wouldn't
'ee?"

Kitty's compassionate nature immediately saw
the situation from Max's point of view. However,
she was not about to give up her ride. There was
only one solution and she smiled kindly at Max
as she offered it. "Then, I must catch up to the
earl and solve the problem." She saw this still did

not satisfy him and frowned. "Does that not settle the matter?"

"Well, the thing is . . . don't know how far ahead 'ee be."

"Oh, I am sure I shall reach him in no time." Kitty laughed softly as she moved to the boot of the coach where her horse was tethered and her sidesaddle safely secured, "Rest easy, Max, I shall be safe enough and riding beside the earl in no time at all."

He scratched his stubbled chin. "Oi suppose . . ."

As Max watched her ride off a few minutes later, he shook his head. He liked Miss Kingsley, truth to tell, he liked her a great deal, though the earl did not seem to like her one bit!

As Kitty trotted her frisky chestnut mare she thought about Max. She didn't think it could be an easy thing to work for someone like the earl. She patted her horse's supple neck, indeed, he must be most exacting, and yet, she had noticed that Max held him in great affection. Odd that.

The earl had been riding at an easy pace, leaving his coach and the ladies at a respectable distance. He had smiled to himself earlier that morning when they had first embarked. He could see that Kitty wanted to ride and he braced himself, ready for a heated debate. However, Miss Diddles was in a talkative mood, excited no doubt about the adventure of their journey and had en-

tered the carriage to pat a place beside herself and
chatter happily. He could see that Kitty simply
could not, would not leave her alone. He had been
momentarily diverted by this observation. It
would appear that Kitty was a kind-hearted little
thing. He had frowned over this, for up until then
he had thought her a willful, spoiled, wild spitfire
of a female with few redeeming qualities.

Then their evening took over his immediate
thoughts. His mind burned with images, pictures
that he found were troubling him more than was
necessary.

Clay wanted Kitty. It was not that Clayton had
been obvious. It was that the earl was experienced
enough to recognize the signs. There was no
doubt in the earl's clear, sharp brain about that
fact. He also knew that while Clay wanted Kitty,
it was Henrietta Harkins Clayton was pursuing in
earnest. No doubt, the young man's pockets were
to let. No doubt, Clay's estates were mortgaged,
and no doubt whatsoever that Clay had no choice,
because to the earl's experienced senses, it was
evident that Clay's interests were not sparked by
desire! Right then, Clayton Bickwerth, like so
many of their class probably had to make a marriage of convenience. Good, that put him out of
Kitty's path. The earl had noticed that she flirted
very prettily with Bickwerth. No no, the earl
shifted in his saddle, that won't do!

Then there was Harry Brentwood. A good lad,
sweet natured, good family. Harry had been at-
tentive to both Kitty and Miss Harkins. He had
displayed no preference in that regard. The earl

smiled to himself. No doubt, the lad simply wanted to be gallant to both young women. However, there was no doubt that when he observed Harry beside Kitty, there seemed to be something special between them. Their lively banter, so easy, so affectionate. Were the two in love with one another? Did their feelings need only a romantic setting to flourish? Should he play cupid and take over the situation? It was ridiculous. What choice had he, though? The terms of his uncle's will required him to see Kitty safely wed. His own conscience dictated that he be certain her future husband be a decent man. Harry was a decent young man of respectable means. Indeed, here was a quick and easy solution to his problem. If he played the game just right, he need not suffer an entire season as Kitty's unwanted guardian. Harry Brentwood was the answer!

Perhaps with some deftness this could be accomplished in the near future. How? What was the next step? Removing Kitty from Harry's immediate vicinity might make the lad realize how he felt about her. That was it, of course, but he could not allow too much time to elapse before he invited Harry to join them in London. These sort of things could go awry. "Hallo?" called an all too familiar, albeit, pretty voice at his back. He spun round, astonished out of his reverie, as Kitty went on to say, "Would you mind some company?" Kitty put on her prettiest smile. She didn't want to fight, and she could see by his expression that he was about to read her a lecture. A little cajolery wouldn't kill her? A voice of logic shouted down her hot temper. "Nanny fell asleep, you see, and I did so need a little air and exercise."

Logic was infectious. He couldn't blame the little minx, after all, he wouldn't want to be forever couped up in a coach on a day such as this? An appreciative smile lit his lush eyes, "I don't mind the company, but I rather thought *you* would."

Kitty laughed and her china blue eyes twinkled. "Flush hit, and I suppose I deserved that. I have been quite dreadful to you, I know. I do not take orders very well, especially from a stranger. I shall try not to be so difficult, if you will try not to be forever ranting and raving the holy proprieties to me. Agreed?"

"Done, my girl. Very soon I shan't have to preach the holy proprieties to you. Minnie will be upon us both, in fact. A great stickler, my Minnie. Rantings and ravings, eh? Mine were nought when pitted against the lashings *she* is capable of administering." He grinned wide and shook his head. "And I must say, my child, if you propose to pitch your gammon at Minnie, you will find yourself checked. I know, I have rarely won a battle with her." He shook his head. "I do, sincerely feel for you, child."

"Faith! You frighten me to the core." Kitty giggled. "Who *is* this Minnie?"

"My grandmother, and a most formidable chaperone, my dear." He was enjoying himself immensely, for he could see that Kitty was, in spite of her amusement, looking somewhat anxious.

"Ah, of course. The dowager. Uncle did speak of her and with a great deal of fondness. I can't imagine *she* is the holy terror you describe." She shook her head. "Never mind, right now, we are *here*, the sky is blue and clear, the footing is excellent, the breeze is lovely, and *I* am itching for a run? Please, oh, do not refuse. Just a short run? Oh, do say we may . . . my lord, and self appointed guardian."

She was a minx. A spritely, vivacious child and damn, how could he resist what he suddenly wanted with all his being? Yes, he wanted to run his horse with her! He smiled broadly and Kitty laughed. He was conscious of the fact that her musical sounds were delightful and a moment later they were cantering down the empty road. They were one in thought as they looked to a hedge separating the road from a wide grassy hill. They laughed joyfully as they fell in stride and took the high jump in unison. They gave their horses full rein, as they careened wildly through the tall grass and up the slope, before coming to a bouncing halt at its peak.

"Oh, lovely. What a fine jumper your horse is. Of course, his timing was at your hands, but he is quite an athlete!" Kit exclaimed happily as she patted her mare's taut neck.

"He is young and has a great deal to learn yet before I take him first flight, but, yes, he is athletic." He inclined his handsome head and said concedingly, "Your own timing, my girl, was perfect. That is a very nice mare. Well mannered as well"

"Thank you," Kitty said breathlessly. Faith, he had such eyes. Rich with color, warm with expression, and his smile was absolutely . . . *stop!* It was the headiness of the moment, that was all.

He ruined all by suggesting then, "I shall ride with you back to the coach, now, Kitty." The use of her name came easily and he liked the feel of it in his throat.

She stiffened and was about to object, but thought better of it and bargained instead. "If you must, I shall not put up a fight, but ask instead that I be allowed another ride later in the day."

He shook his head. "I think not. You see— "

"Really?" Kitty interrupted as she lost her control, "Why the deuce not?"

"Because very soon we shall be on the busiest part of this road and it won't do."

"Oh won't it?" Kitty retorted, "Well, we shall see."

" 'You will obey me in this," he countered, much incensed.

"Do you think so?" returned the lady.

"I know so, spitfire. Believe me, I know so," he answered and though Kitty's blue eyes glinted defiantly, she managed to keep still. Her mind worked feverishly though, and thus, their peace was temporarily at an end!

Fourteen

Miss Diddles was wide awake and chattering happily about the passing scenery, totally unaware that Kitty scarcely heard a word. Kitty had other things on her mind. Chiefly being, the need to formulate a plan designed to serve the earl for his harsh, unfeeling treatment of her earlier. In the meantime, two hours had dragged by since the earl had deposited her in the coach and rode off. Two hours, for goodness sake. It was the outside of enough, that a man could do whatever he dashed well wanted to do, while women had to endure their dictums!

Did *he* care about their comfort? Obviously he did not! Did he not think that she and Nanny might wish to stretch their legs or have a bite to eat? After all, it had been *four,* maybe nearly five hours since they had left Warton. What of the horses? Indeed, forget about poor Nanny who might need a respite from traveling, but what of all the horses?

All at once, their carriage slowed to a halt and even as Kitty got ready to have a look and see what was towards, the coach door opened to display the earl. Kitty's heart raced with sure feelings, all of them heated. The earl's hazel eyes twinkled, but he did not direct himself to her as he smiled, and tipped his hat to say, "Miss Diddles. I thought I would avail myself of the pleasure of your company for the next half hour or so, if you and Miss Kingsley wouldn't mind?"

"Mind? Why I am certain I have bored my poor girl to tears, prattling on and on about absolutely nothing. Please do sit with us and bear us company." Miss Diddles smiled softly.

Ah, thought Kit, he is back to calling me Miss Kingsley. Really, one would think *he* had been offended? Fine, so he means to take that road? Right . . . "Saddle sore, my lord?" Kitty asked sweetly and her blue eyes glittered.

"Kitty!" objected Nanny with a small twitter. "Kitty loves to tease, my lord, but, I am certain you have already noticed that."

"Indeed, I have." He smiled at Miss Diddles, and turned to give Kitty a wry look and answer her comment, "Not saddle sore, child, I am used to long hours in the saddle. However, there is a very lovely inn about five or so miles down the road. I thought we might rest the horses there and take an hour to enjoy a luncheon."

"Oh, how very thoughtful." Miss Diddles sighed. "I must confess, that I should dearly love a spot of tea."

"Well I should like a sight more than tea and have been half famished for the last hour, my lord," stuck in Kitty aware that she sounded like a spoiled brat. However, as she shot a reproving glance his way, she was surprised to note that he had taken her petty words to heart and felt a twinge of guilt.

"Indeed, I have been most remiss. Forgive me for not having realized sooner that both of you might need a stop."

"Woosh!" Nanny waved this off. "Your timing is perfect." She turned a determined look upon Kitty. "Isn't it, dear?"

"Why, of course. And the sun is the moon. Isn't that how it goes?" riposted Kitty as graciousness eluded her.

To her astonishment, the earl burst into mirth in which her nanny nervously joined. "Ah, that is my girl, forever teasing."

Kitty reluctantly smiled. "That is what I do on an empty stomach. I tease."

"I shall be sure to keep you fed, in the future, spitfire, you may depend upon it," chuckled the earl.

"Ah, afraid of my country bumpkin wit, eh, my lord?" pursued Kitty on the offense, and enjoying herself immensely. At least, when she was with the earl, there was no denying that she felt alive!

"Wit, is it? Od's life, child, arrant manners, but quite engaging, all the same."

"Now that is a bang up thing to say. Famous! I amuse you. Should I be flattered, my lord?"

Nanny clucked her tongue and admonished softly, "Kitty, Kitty."

However, though the earl cast Kitty a disparaging glance, he glibly, and skillfully dodged her quip, by quietly pointing out, "Ah, the Red Lion. At last."

Diverted, Kitty excitedly looked away from him to scan their new surroundings. The window in the carriage afforded her an excellent view as the carriage turned off the main road onto a neatly cobbled courtyard ablaze with potted daffodils and cleanly trimmed evergreens.

"Oh," Kitty admired openly. "How quaint. Nanny, only look at all the flowers. Look there, tulips!"

"Lovely, dear, lovely."

The carriage had come to a complete stop and as a bevy of young ostlers rushed to the horses' heads, Max came round and opened the carriage door wide. The earl nimbly alighted first and turned to give his hand first to Miss Diddles who stood aside to shake out her grey traveling ensemble. He turned then to Kitty and his hazel eyes twinkled for he could see that she did not wish to give him her hand. However, as Kitty stepped down, the hem of her skirt caught on the coach door hinge. She felt the tug on her skirt, looked round, lost her balance and went tripping forward. The earl caught her deftly in his arms, and for a long moment held her firmly. Blue eyes looked up and found hazel eyes alight with mischievous amber lights. Kitty was conscious of a new most foreign tingle of excitement. She found herself blushing as she breathed, "Thank you. I only hope I haven't torn my gown."

"Don't move," he answered as he reached round and bent to release her skirt from the doorway. "There. I don't believe it has been damaged." The earl's voice was soft and almost mesmerizing.

Kitty felt as though she couldn't breathe. What was this? Stop, she told herself. What was this foolishness? Yet, she was momentarily taken aback, by this new, almost seductive side to the complex Earl of Halloway. Somehow, and all at once, he released his hold on her and in some confusion she stepped away. *Just what was this?* However, Kitty had no time to contemplate this fresh discovery, for the stillness of the moment was suddenly broken by the sound of her name resonantly hitting the air in merry accents, "Kitten, my own little Kitten!"

Kitty looked up, and past the earl's broad shoulder, at a tall, well dressed Corinthian coming towards her, "Alex! Oh, Alex!" she called and danced toward him.

Lord Magdalen picked Kitty up and spun her round in full view of the earl who had turned sharply at the sound of a most familiar voice.

As Magdalen jostled Kitty and told her she had grown into a beauty, the earl's defined dark brows were up and his voice, when he spoke was decidedly dry, "Dearest Alex, best of my friends, I always allow you more license than others. Even so, I *must* ask you to unhand my ward."

Magdalen looked round from his appraisal of Kitty, and in great astonishment ejaculated, "George! By all the Saints! What the devil are you doing in these parts?" And then before his friend could answer, "Ward? What in blazes are you saying?" Then as dawning lit in his dark grey eyes, "Ward? Lud! Do you mean . . ." He turned to

Kitty and held her hands. "Kitten, never say the old fellow is gone?"

Kitty nodded sadly. "For just over a month."

Magdalen patted her shoulder and then followed this up with a strong hug. "There, there, poor child. But how do you come to be in this rogue's company? And where is Nanny?"

"Here, my lord," said Miss Diddles coming from the boot of the coach where she had been extracting something from one of her traveling bags. She put out her hand and enveloped Magdalen with a warm smile. "How nice to see you looking as lively as ever."

"She means, looking as devilish as ever, but is too polite to say so," teased Kitty.

"But, you, are not polite in the least, are you Kitten?" Magdalen returned amiably as he flicked her nose. He frowned then, and pursued, "Still, what does Rogue Halloway mean, calling you his ward?"

Kitty sighed, "Well . . ."

"Because, in a manner of speaking that is precisely what I am, but I rather think we should take this conversation indoors," interrupted the earl, who found himself taking Kitty's elbow. This left Magdalen to good naturedly offer Nanny his arm and happily bring up the rear, as he called out loudly for the innkeeper and ordered them a private parlor. This done, he turned to the earl and snorted. "Now we may be private and you may explain this havey cavey affair to me."

* * *

Just as the Earl of Halloway's lively group sat to lunch at the Red Lion, Lady Jersey stood up from her yellow satin chair and set her dainty china teacup down on the small Hepplewhite side table. Deep in thought, she took a slow turn around the elegantly furnished parlor of Halloway House and came to stand with the wide bowed window overlooking the quiet square at her back. She rarely allowed the sun to shine full on her face anymore. She had been an attractive, almost beautiful young woman, but though many still called her lovely, she knew her age was beginning to show.

Well, well, this certainly was an odd turn of events indeed, she thought curiously as the dowager continued to chatter amiably in the background. Just how should she handle this matter? The earl was a favorite flirt of hers, indeed, if she were not sleeping with the Prince Regent, she would have dallied her way into the Earl of Halloway's bed. He was so very magnetic, and the fact that he was years younger made no difference to her. She smiled softly as she thought of the earl and then sighed. His grandmother, Minerva, was a highly respected and extremely influential former London hostess. She patted the dark hair at her ear and pursed her lips. Still, she must make a token show of power, "Well, the thing is Minnie, she is not even related to you, and we don't make a habit of issuing vouchers without first meeting— "

Minnie waved this off as she interrupted Sally Jersey, "Don't be absurd. Were you not listening to me, dear? I told you, she is a Kingsley! Her father was the second son of the Baron Kingsley, and her mother was one of old Bennings' daughters. Nothing to scoff at there. Besides, she is under *my* protection. I expect vouchers to arrive here before she does."

Lady Jersey was not only a handsome woman, she was far too clever to insult the Countess of Halloway. She gracefully inclined her head, "Of course, Minnie darling, as you say, she is a Kingsley. Very excellent breeding there. And she is, I suppose an heiress if she was Warton's ward?"

Minnie was well acquainted with the Jersey. She knew well just how malicious the woman could be. One could not be too careful, and there was no need for her to know more than she should, "I would not call her quite an heiress. Suffice it to say, that her dowry is more than respectable, and her competence not unattractive. My grandson, George, was Warton's nephew, and as such, inherited the estate and quite a sizable fortune as well." There, no need for Sally Jersey to know the *particular* details of that absurd will. No need, whatsoever!

"Did he?" mused one of the biggest gossips in all of the Beau Monde. The Jersey mulled this over a moment. "I suppose that makes dearest George a marriage prize indeed. La! A title, good looks, charm and wealth. Well, well . . . this should be an interesting season." Lady Jersey tittered meaningfully. "Minnie, darling, no doubt you will soon be presiding over two weddings!"

"Indeed," remarked the dowager countess gritting her teeth. "Wouldn't that be lovely."

Fifteen

Magdalen pushed his empty plate away. "I can not eat anymore."

"Well that is very good, since you have eaten everything in sight!" giggled Kitty very much at ease with the baron. Magdalen was, like the earl, seven-and-twenty years old, but he was a longtime friend of Kitty's. As he had explained earlier to the more than interested earl, one of his smaller, but successful estates, his Beaulieu Manor, ran only a few miles away from Warton Castle. He had inherited Beaulieu when he first left Cambridge. He had discovered Kitty in that same year when he came down to hunt with the Beaulieu Hounds. She was riding with the huntsman when he had first spotted her. A plucky little thing, helping the whips keep a few wayward young hounds off the scent of deer. Kitty had been twelve, and he had been twenty-one, but that hadn't stopped her from barking at him when his horse nearly kicked a hound that had ventured too close,

"A mad little hoyden, ready to take on the world." Magdalen concluded his story and then had eyed the earl thoughtfully. "But, aye then, Halloway, you must have noticed that by now?"

The earl had not answered him then, and now as he watched his friend dally charmingly with both Nanny and Kitty, it occurred to him that Kitty was really quite an innocent. She was not at all up to snuff and characters like Magdalen could easily have her for a snack if he did not watch out. Indeed, Magdalen had sent quite a few maidens into a decline.

"So then, Alex, you didn't say, are you on your way to your Beaulieu Manor now?" The earl asked tentatively as he sipped his cordial.

"No, I just spent a few nights visiting friends not far from Winchester. On my way to London, like you." He gave Kitty a wide grin.

"Prime!" ejaculated Kitty with a clap of her hands, "Then I shall have a friendly face in the crowd."

Magdalen laughed. "Yes, pet, a friendly one indeed." He flicked her nose. "You must tell me when you grew up? The last time I looked you were a babe, and that was not so *very* long ago?"

"It was too!" declared Kitty. "It has been a year, an entire year, and then we only met briefly."

"Far *too* briefly," said Magdalen on a low note. He was an experienced rake who knew the game well. He was not deterred by the fact that Kitty did not know the game at all.

"Well," said the earl all at once, "I am sorry to break up this happy reunion, but, I am afraid we should be on our way."

"I will travel with you," announced Magdalen.

The earl looked at him for a long moment and said quietly, "I rather thought you would."

Magdalen understood the message that was given in that look and laughed. "Ah, to see you in this role, my sweet Halloway, does wonders for my soul. There is hope for me yet."

"If you behave, Alex, if you behave, there is hope," said the earl clapping his friend on the shoulder.

The truth was that he and Alex had often enjoyed an evening of devilry, and ribald pleasures. He liked Alex, but they were made of different fibers. The earl was often restricted by his code of honour. Alex took the code to the limit, and in this they were totally divergent. Alex did not give a fig about the ethics of fair play that were the basis of all of the earl's final decisions. To Alex, winning, having, doing was all there was. No, thought the earl, he would not allow Alex to bring her low. She was far too vulnerable for the likes of Magdalen!

The carriage was brought round as was Magdalen's horse some moments later. Kitty was surprised to hear the baron order the groom to tether his horse with the others at the boot of the earl's coach.

Halloway pulled a face. "I don't think that is a good idea, Alex. It will be a tight fit for the three horses."

"Aye. Leave Bouncer on a long line. He'll do. Good sort, Bouncer."

The earl's eyes narrowed thoughtfully as he watched Magdalen laugh and climb into the coach after the ladies. No, no, my friend, the earl decided as he climbed in after him.

"Well, this is cozy." Magdalen grinned satanically his grey eyes caressing Kitty.

Kitty, was not quite as green as the earl feared. She had over the last few years watched Magdalen in action both on and off the hunting field. She had seen quite clearly during that time that he really liked the ladies, all the ladies, but, she also saw that he didn't like them enough to care about what happened to them when he walked away. She had heard the whispers about him quite a long time ago. She was fully aware that he was a superficial, albeit, captivating cavalier, quite heedlessly capable of ruining a virgin whether she be barmaid, chambermaid or green country miss. She had observed him closely, curious because he had seemed so hero-like at first. Wise beyond her experience, she detected a certain self-serving insincerity in his style. When both Harry and her dear, late guardian issued very clear statements regarding Magdalen's character, she absorbed and understood their meaning.

Barring that, she enjoyed Alex, and she was both flattered and bolstered by his attention, but she was not fooled. However, she meant to play his game, if only to annoy the earl, for she could see that the earl was annoyed by Magdalen's intrusion. Why this was so, she could not fathom. After all, the earl wanted as little to do with her as possible. He should be pleased to find himself unburdened.

The next two hours were spent quite pleasantly

as Magdalen kept them entertained with a series of lively anecdotes. Once or twice, the earl had managed a smile, but for the most part, he maintained a quiet vigil, except to answer one or two queries Nanny put to him. Then all at once, the earl signaled for Max to halt the coach, "I beg your pardon; we are just coming up to Hartly where there is a very elegant posting house. I mean to ride ahead and procure us some rooms for the evening, and a private chamber for our dinner. It will soon be getting dark and I don't think we should ask any more of the horses."

Magdalen looked out the window. "No doubt, we are stopping at the Hartly Inn." He turned to the ladies and as though it had all been his own doing, he announced, "Capital spot, the Hartly. Landscaped gardens, very pretty. You'll like the Hartly."

The earl inclined his head. "Right you are, Alex. The Hartly it is." He felt very much like throttling Magdalen, but kept himself in check. Damn, when had he gotten so somber? He felt like a conservative old man! He had never put so much thought into his travels, and in fact, he had Max go slightly out of their way so that he could select an inn the ladies might enjoy. What did it matter? Well, it did. That was all he knew.

Kitty was fully aware of the earl's irritation, and in fairness to him, she admitted to herself that Magdalen had monopolized the conversation and had done so without including the earl. Even now, Magdalen was seemingly taking credit for the earl's plan to stop at what was apparently a very fine posting house. She watched the earl jump down from the carriage steps and as he turned, their eyes met. For some unknown reason she felt a moment's uncertainty. She frowned at Magdalen. After all, why should the earl have to do everything by himself? Well, no doubt, Alex thought he was doing the gentlemanly thing by remaining with the ladies. It was strange to think of Magdalen and the earl as friends. She could see that they were both Corinthians, and no doubt, enjoyed many of the same pleasures. Still, they were so very different.

Outside and on horseback, the earl silently fumed. In the past, he had often found himself competing with Magdalen for a female's attention. There had been, Lady Caro, only just recently. He smiled to himself. That was different. Caro knew the rules and in the end, she had played fast and loose, forsaking him, and her husband, for Lord Byron!

That was the heart of the matter. The females he and Alex had often sported to win had always been experienced ladies, quite ready and able to play the game. Kitty Kingsley had nought to do with any of that! For all practical purposes, Kitty was his ward and under his protection. That put a very different shade on the matter. He couldn't very well vie with Alex for Kitty's attention, and thus, he had found himself sitting back and allowing Magdalen to play gallant during their ride. He patted his horse's neck and said, "That can not continue." No, damnation, it could not! But he had apparently left the avenue wide open for Alex to move in and take over. Indeed, he had been left at a definite disadvantage. He could warn Kitty off Magdalen. No, she wouldn't heed him. The sorry fact was that Kitty seemed to hold him in sure contempt. He wondered about that. What exactly had he done to bring that about? He shook his head, more than a little exasperated with the situation. Never mind, soon he would put his ward in Minnie's capable hands and be done with her! A curse softly touched his lips, "Damn Magdalen's eyes!"

Sixteen

London with all its bustle enveloped the Halloway carriage as it ambled into the city's thriving heart. Kitty was nearly hanging out the window as she watched hawkers offer their various wares. An urchin called out in a resonant voice as their carriage passed him by, "Hot house strawberries. Here there be. Ripe. Hot house strawberries."

Kitty smiled at him as they went by and nearly called for Max to halt the coach and buy a basket of the luscious looking fruit. However, she was stalled by Nanny who fussed and pulled her back against the squabs to declare, "What then, love. Should we be greeting the Countess of Halloway with a basket of strawberries in our hands and looking country foolish?"

Kitty laughed and sighed. "I suppose you are right, but is it not all so amazing? So very different than what I remember."

" 'Tis the same, love. It is you that is different," Nanny offered affectionately.

Kitty sat back to consider this. She had been to London so many times as a young child with her parents, but couldn't recall very much from those days. However, her late guardian had brought her

into the city when she was twelve and she had not
liked the restrictions that had accompanied her
time there. Now, there was definitely something
different that caught her adult curiosity and tickled her senses. A contrary notion that now she just
might well fit in, made her overwhelmed with a
measure of excitement. Once more she was peer-
ing avidly out her carriage window.

Fashionable ladies glided by. "Oh, Nanny, look
at their *clothes!*"

"Yes dear, very pretty." Nanny smiled.

Dandies wearing fashion at its extreme walked
and waved to one another and Kitty giggled.
"Nanny. Nanny, there, dandies on the strut!"

"Darling, your language! You can't go repeating the sort of things you can only have learned
from dearest Harry. He should not have talked
that way in your presence."

Kitty paid this no heed, but satisfied with her
first view of London, she sat back with a thump
and a bounce of sheer energy against the squabs
of the comfortable seat and sighed wistfully. Well,
this Season, she thought to herself, should prove
a great deal more interesting than she had hith-
erto imagined. With that thought, her mind wan-
dered back to Magdalen and their dinner together
the previous evening.

The earl had been a perfect host, even jovial.
After she and Nanny had refreshed themselves in
a room that was both huge and beautifully deco-
rated, they joined the gentlemen in a private parlor. There, they found the earl and Magdalen
enjoying their brandy and in high spirits. This

mood carried them through a sumptuous dinner. She could have stayed all night to watch the earl and Magdalen as they engaged one another in an entertaining banter. However, Nanny insisted they retire. Kitty could see that it was the correct thing to do, after all, they were in a public house.

Magdalen took her hand and bent low over it. She had the distinct notion that he was in his cups as he softly but almost on a slur said, "May your dreams be of me, and keep you warm, my pretty Kitten." He audaciously kissed her wrist. Kitty's brow went up and for a moment she felt the earl tense angrily. Indeed, if the earl really regarded her as his ward, she could perfectly understand his finding his cavalier friend's outrageous behavior quite over the limit. In fact, she was not quite pleased with Magdalen. Did he think she would swoon at his feet, like a green country twit? However, she took no real offense.

Hurriedly she said, in order to avoid any trouble, "You are very naughty, Alex, but we know each other so well that I shall not heed it." Thus, she had the satisfaction of actually seeing the earl suddenly relax. She had not realized he could be so easily mollified in her regard. She had thought him much more cantankerous. She then hurriedly took Nanny's arm and led her away.

Well, there was no doubt now that Magdalen spent most of the remainder of his night imbibing enough to make him sleep for a week. The earl met them at the prescribed hour of seven in the morning with the intelligence that Magdalen would be traveling the remaining miles to London, later in the day, and on his own.

Kitty had asked pertly, "Oh? Why is that?"

The earl chuckled and flicked her nose. "A knowing one I have on my hands, eh? Well, then, it's nothing more than sleep the old boy needs. He'll do." The earl could scarcely hide his smirk before he turned his face away from her curious scrutiny.

She could still see his profile and noted that the smile still lighted in his eyes as he advised them that he would be taking to horse.

Kitty made a feeble objection. "Oh, now that is very unfair, indeed. Here we have another glorious spring day and I am so used to morning rides." The plea was in her blue eyes.

"You may have your morning rides in Hyde Park once you are established in London. For now, let us not have any arguments. I must ride on ahead to make certain all is in readiness for your arrival."

Kitty decided to accept this in good stead and lowered her lashes as she controlled a rebuttal. He laughed and touched her chin. "What, Kitty, no fight left?"

Her blue eyes flashed at that and he put up his hands. "Spare me, child, I am off!"

Well, that had been at least three hours ago and now here they were in London! She had not wanted to come here. There had been no thoughts of London, or a London Season in her mind. She had been happy, content in the New Forest at Warton. So then, why did she feel so thrilled to be here now? She asked herself this, and then did not bother to worry about an answer as suddenly, the bustle of the streets was left at their backs as their coach turned off Brompton.

Kitty turned to Nanny and excitedly declared, "We must be getting close!"

Nanny had a look around and gave it as her opinion that, indeed, it wouldn't be much longer.

This proved quite true for, Kitty could see the wide green of the park and exclaimed, "There, that is Hyde Park. I remember it. Uncle Edwin took me there. That is the Serpentine! Kensington can't be far now." She sighed and gave Nanny a long thoughtful look. "You know, I don't think I shall absolutely *hate* being here in London."

"I know, dear. 'Tis not in your nature to hate anything, but to make the best of everything. Such a stout heart you have." So saying, Nanny affectionately touched her charge's rosy cheek.

"Oh, Nanny, I love you." Kitty snuggled her for a moment and then the carriage pulled to a stop!

Halloway House was an impressive work of stone, colonnades and spiked black iron railing both on the first floor and at the long balcony of the second and third floor. Its first floor housed two of the newly popular bow windows, only just installed. A set of moulded doors beneath a wide canopy set off the entire facade, and the total effect was most impressive.

Nanny thanked Max as she held his sturdy arm and took a step gingerly away from the carriage. As she turned she shook her head to watch Kitty amiably take Max's hand and skip down the steps. "Max, this looks very grand. Has the earl been living here all alone?"

"Aw naw, 'is lordship 'as bachelor lodgings not too far from 'ere." He smiled broadly. "This 'ere 'ouse as been closed now for jest about two years. The dowager she took to living year round at the Grange ye see . . ." His attention was caught and he suddenly motioned to the front door as Wilson, the butler, held it open wide. "Aye then, Oi see that they be waiting on ye, so Oi'll jest go taike the 'orses to the stables and get them bedded down."

Kitty absorbed this as she took Nanny's hand and moved toward the front stone steps. Suddenly, she felt herself quake. What if the dowager took her in dislike? What if she didn't have enough social grace to make an initial impression? What if she made a fool of herself and disgraced the Halloways? Oh, faith! How would she know what she must do and what she must not? Oh no, her time had come for there, standing right before her, was the dowager herself!

Minerva, Countess of Halloway, stood just inside the wide marbled entranceway. It was an imposing setting, with a collage of rich though darkly cast paintings, of what could only be Halloway ancestors, all properly proud, covering the left wall. Flanking her on the right was a wainscotted wall completely dominated by an enormous gold framed mirror and a Sheraton side table, richly painted with floral wreaths. At the lady's regal back were highly polished mahogany stairs covered with an Oriental runner. All of these things made a perfectly intimidating setting for a young girl already in a quake. While it was true that Warton Castle had its own noble history, it was not Kitty's very own. She had lost her parents while she was too young to have attained a sense of family heritage. She was most certainly overwhelmed.

The countess's attention had momentarily been diverted by a footman, who had appeared with the luggage, enabling Kitty to observe everything in a quick blur. She watched too, how Minerva managed her servants, firmly, but with a sure aura of kindness. Then, all at once, the lady came forward, taking all Kitty's absorption.

"Welcome . . . welcome . . ." Kitty heard the dowager countess say as she felt Minerva appraise her.

"Thank you." Kitty continued to study her hostess. She could see that she was certainly of goodly height and substantial figure. Seventy years old? Kitty thought she looked much younger than seventy. Perhaps it was the rich blue velvet gown trimmed with a pretty white lace collar. Perhaps it was the way her grey, wispy curls escaped the knot at the top of her head, fringing what was now a lively, and what had once been, quite a taking, though not classically beautiful, countenance. Or maybe it was her eyes?

"Dear, dear, what can that grandson of mine

have said of me, to make you stand there? Come, child, I shan't eat you. I promise."

Kitty laughed. "Sure? I am, though I was told that was the fate of all green country girls in London."

The countess was surprised into a genuine cackle of mirth.

"But you ain't so green, are you, child?" She turned then immediately to Nanny and smiled warmly. "You must be, Miss Diddles. My grandson tells me you are an estimable woman, but I fear he has misused you. Tch, tch, forcing that trip on you in just two days!" She put a hand to her cheek. "I only hope you are not fagged to death."

Miss Diddles mumbled shyly, "Oh no, his lordship was everything that was kind and considerate."

"Really? You give me cause for hope then." She smiled and linked her arm through Kitty's. "Come, there is a blazing fire awaiting us in the library where we shall sit and enjoy a cozy tea."

"Is the earl not here?" Kitty managed to ask curiously.

"Ah, no my dear. Won't I do for the time being?"

"Far better," started Kitty and then blushed hotly. "Ah . . . I mean . . ."

Minnie laughed. "Never mind, you need not guard your tongue with me, child. No, indeed, for we are going to be great friends."

Seventeen

The earl entered White's and found himself clapped on the shoulder by several of his sporting friends. One fellow, Lord Rodhill smirked slightly as he demanded, "What's this? Hear you've inherited an incredible fortune."

"So I'm told," said the earl dryly. He did not like Rodhill and took no trouble to hide the fact.

"Aye," Rodhill pursued as he took a sip of port. "A fortune, indeed, from all accounts."

The earl's brow was up with the challenge. He and Rodhill were ever at odds over one thing or another. The fellow was a jackanapes and the earl fancied he knew just where this was going. He answered, his eyes narrowed warningly. "Your . . . er . . . point, my lord? Or do you just like to hear yourself go on about money? I can understand that, for *I* understand you lost a hale sum on that last pony you backed."

A round of laughter sprang up, for the nag Rodhill had backed to win had come in dead last and lame. His lordship flushed and said, "No matter. I shall recover, but you, my lord, I don't suppose you will have time for such pleasures while playing . . . what shall we call what you are to your new acquisition, eh?" He shook his head. "Tut, tut . . . imagine making *you* sole protector . . . to a *miss*, just out of the schoolroom?"

The room went silent, and indeed, Rodhill, himself went white for a moment, wondering if he had gone too far. The earl was a noted marksman, and Rodhill had no wish to find himself facing him in the morning!

"Protector is a very good term, indeed," said the earl, his hazel eyes glinting fire. "Guardian, is a better one. However, my ward is not solely in my charge, but quite safely in the hands of my grandmother, Lady Halloway."

"Of course, of course," said Rodhill with a flip of his hand, "One assumed as much."

"Excellent, then perhaps we may move on to more interesting topics. What news is there of Napoleon?"

After they had enjoyed a friendly chat, imbibed a good deal of hot tea and devoured a delectable assortment of miniature cakes and small squares of buttered bread, Kitty sat back to watch the countess with growing respect, as that worthy woman whisked Miss Diddles off, adjuring her to enjoy a leisurely hot bath and then a long nap in her room. At the library door, however, Lady Hallaway relinquished Nanny to a chambermaid's care, and turned to announce briskly, "Well, child, now, you and I are going on a shopping spree from which, we shall not return until we are thoroughly exhausted."

Kitty laughed. "Shopping, now?"

"Never say, *you* are too fatigued from your journey?" Minnie snorted dubiously.

"No, no . . . but . . ."

Minnie cast a deprecating eye over Kitty's new royal blue habit which was travel-worn from two days use, "Look here, child, I mean for you to take the Beau Monde by storm, and you certainly can not do so in *clothes* like that!" She clucked her tongue. "None of your things, will do!"

Kitty laughed. "But my lady, you haven't even seen my other things?"

"*I* don't have to. They were not made by Madame Toussard." She then wagged a finger. "And I have already asked you to call me Minnie. Please do so, it will make us so very comfy together. Now, come along."

It was late afternoon, but, Bond Street was bustling still, very much alive, with men and women patronizing their favorite shops.

Kitty was, in fact, in a shop, run by a French woman acknowledged by the haute ton as a modiste of the first stare. She stood, in her bare feet and a silk wrapper madame had given her to wear between fittings, in a private room overlooking the street, and wondered if she would ever recognize herself in the new fashionable gowns they were moulding to her body. It was all so very strange and wonderful. Who would ever have thought that she, the hoyden of Warton, would ever have loved the feel and look of such exquisite fabrics? She, who had always been happy in her buckskins and woolens?

She crossed the room and slumped wearily onto the window seat to laugh. "Enough. No more. I can't look at another gown." The countess had by this time been totally captivated by Kitty. Minerva had been sadly blue-deviled after her ward, Shawna, had married nearly a year ago. It was what she had wanted, but, still it had left her lonely. Kitty's lively companionship was a soothing balm for her ailing spirits. "Nonsense, I want to try the white against your skin."

"No, no, that could only be made into something missy and frilly," objected Kitty.

"Not *that*, you goose. As though *I* would pick out such as that? The sheer silk with the gold dust throughout."

"Oh, yes, but that was so dear."

"Your solicitor arranged a carte blanche voucher for your entire season. No expense is to be spared. Now, I think white slippers, not gold—"

"Oh, yes. But some white ribbons with the gold trim. Yes, yes, it will be stunning."

"Which reminds me, I must have Jacques come to you first thing tomorrow morning."

"Who is Jacques and why must he come to me first thing in the morning?"

"Jacques? There is no one who can wield a pair of scissors and a comb, like Jacques. Your hair, my child, must be cut, must be styled."

"Cut? You want to cut my hair." Kitty nearly

shrieked, "No, no, it took years to get it to reach my waist."

"Kitty, you have so much hair, so thick. We need to cut only here and there, you will see." Minnie was in a high fettle. "Now, cloaks. This deep blue velvet, with a white gauze trim around the hood. Black velvet cloak with a red lining. And, madame, another in white velvet with gold . . ."

Madame was in ecstasy, not only because of the amount of the sale, but because it always gave her great pleasure to design for and fit a new ingenue, especially one who showed promise of unique beauty. Besides, dressing one connected to a Halloway could only add to her already considerable consequence in the World of Modistes!

Kitty laughed and closed her eyes. Where was she? This was like a fairy tale. She couldn't believe how fast everything was taking place. It was at that moment, that a familiar voice, though somewhat muffled by distance, caught her attention. The voices came from just outside the window? Kitty peeped between the brocade curtains and saw the earl. He was standing with a fashionably dressed, and extremely lovely red-haired woman. Fascinated she watched as the woman touched his firm chin. Amazed at this public display, Kitty's mouth dropped. Intrigued, Kitty watched the woman audaciously purse her lips for a quick kiss. She could just barely hear the woman say, "Have you been avoiding me, darling George? I haven't seen you in an age. Just when I thought we might get . . . closer . . . you were gone." There was no mistaking the meaning in her eyes, her tone and her carefully chosen words.

Kitty was astounded. She watched the earl take the woman's soft kid gloved hands, and kiss her fingertips. Kitty saw the devilish glance he gave her as he brought his head back up to say, "I can not think of anything I could want more— "

"*Kitty!*" objected Minnie. "What *are* you doing? You must not be seen at the window." So saying, she took a peek herself, "Eh, my grandson, is it? Making a spectacle of himself with Mrs. Saltash! Humph!"

"Is that . . . a special friend of the earl's?" Kitty could not refrain from asking.

"Ha! Special friend indeed! Well, never mind," answered Minnie as she turned away from the window. "Madame is ready for you, and we must hurry if we are to get to the milliners."

The earl watched Felicia Saltash sway as she moved down the avenue. A very desirable piece of fluff, he thought, but, dangerous, so extremely dangerous. She was ton, perhaps not the pink of ton, but, nevertheless toying with a widow of his own class could end with him at the altar. Damn! The very notion of being tied forever to Felicia Saltash made him tremble. He was well out of her clutches! He turned away with a regretful sigh, only to find, bearing down on him, with sure purpose, Alex, Lord Magdalen, who had only just arrived in London.

"George." Magdalen hailed him, but with a smile.

"Ah, Alex. Head any better?"

"Egad, no, how could it be after all the brandy you plied me with last night?"

"I ply *you*? My dear, Alex, whenever have *I* had to persuade you to drink?" chuckled the earl.

"Last night was a bit different, my lad. Meant to cut me out this morning, admit it! Truth be, I would have done the same to you, had our positions been reversed." He shrugged this off. "No harm. Have an entire season ahead of us, don't *we*?" This last was sweetly said, but there was no doubt as to his intentions.

"The thing is, Alex, the emphasis, you must keep in mind, is on the word *we,* in the Season ahead. Wither thou goest, my buck . . . and so on . . ." drawled the earl and the glint was in his hazel eyes.

"Pity. Your delicious ward does make my heart throb, you know, but, I have no wish to step on a friend's toe. Since you have thrust them, your toes, that is, in my way, I bow to our friendship and stand aside."

"I have never thought you, unwise, Alex." Halloway grinned, "Now, shall I find you later tonight at White's?"

"No . . . no . . . tonight I am opera bound . . ." He smiled rakishly, "Where I mean to steal the pretty Felicia right out from under you." He winked as he moved off. "Compensation, my boy, compensation!"

Eighteen

Kitty awoke to find a young chambermaid drawing the ivory brocade hangings. A bright sun, shadowed only by scudding irregular capes of white, displayed itself and demanded her attention. "Oh for goodness sake! What have I done?" Kitty had been introduced to the bright-eyed maid, the night before. "Bess, what time is it?" However, even as she asked, her blue eyes glanced towards the brass encased clock reposing sedately on the marbled mantle of her fireplace. "Nine! Faith, nine o'clock." Kitty's eyes opened wide. "Wicked, I feel so wicked. How did I sleep through the morning?"

"Bless ye, miss," Bess giggled. "The morning has just begun. My lady won't be up and about for another hour yet."

"Well, *my* mornings normally begin much earlier." Kitty smiled. She slipped out of her four poster bed, pulled on her well worn slippers and moved to her window. This overlooked the quiet garden. There were tulips in bloom, as well as daffodils in scalloped flower beds. Large evergreens were trimmed and shaped in huge boxes of earth and set between benches. Larger evergreens and towering, newly-budding trees reposed against the tall stone wall that encased the garden.

As Bess poured Kitty a cup of tea, the bedroom door opened just a crack and Miss Diddles peered in to say, "Ah, you *are* up! I am so glad." She turned then to a young woman who looked to be in her early thirties. The woman was respectably clothed in crisp blue linen. A neat white mop cap covered a head of soft brown hair, gathered tightly at the nape of her neck with a white ribbon. Short wispy bangs fanned her forehead. Rosy cheeks and bright brown eyes gave her a robust, healthy appearance. Kitty immediately smiled a welcome as Nanny brought the woman into the room. "Say hello to Mrs. Wilson, Kitty. The dowager has just this morning appointed her to be your dresser, my dear."

"My dresser?" Kitty laughed. "Well, I am very pleased to have you. Lady Halloway must have guessed my great need. I had not the least notion how I was to dress myself in those lovely clothes we purchased yesterday, without help. I do hope you will be patient with me, Wilson. I was wont to be a country hoyden, free of fashion's absurdities!"

Her naive speech immediately endeared her to Mrs. Wilson, whose skill as a dresser was deft, and her experience varied. She had worked as a ladies' personal maid for the debutante daughters of some of the more famous noble houses over the last decade and was well known in her own circle. Few were quicker or more skilled with a needle for a quick tuck here and a mend there. She was neat with a brush and comb and had the knack of dressing hair with expertise. The countess had been delighted when the Wilsons, who had been serving in different households had agreed to come to work for her.

Mrs. Wilson found Halloway House and the quarters she shared with her husband there most comfortable. More than that, within moments of meeting her, she realized she genuinely liked her new young lady.

It wasn't just what Kitty had said to her upon their meeting. It had been the sweet smile which had accompanied Kitty's words that had distinguished her from her predecessors and softened Mrs. Wilson's critical heart. She had dressed many aristocratic, young, lovely, and wealthy maids, but this one was quite different. At least upon first meeting. A sensible woman, Mrs. Wilson decided that she would reserve her opinion to time, ever the truthsayer.

And then Kitty sealed her first impression, "Wilson? Oh, how lovely, you must be Wilson's wife! How perfect this is, for now we all may be comfortable!" Kitty had always been an odd mixture of romantic and pragmatic.

"Well, miss, that is why her ladyship chose me for this office." Mrs. Wilson was, wisely, a woman of few words with strangers.

Thus, it was an hour later, after Kitty had bathed and been clothed in a morning gown of

soft mint green, trimmed at its heart shape neckline with a single flounce of cream-colored
worked lace, that Kitty emerged from her room
feeling much like a princess in a fairy tale. Her
hair had been fashionably clipped, shaped and set
in glorious ringlets of gold at the top of her well
shaped head, giving her additional height. When
she left her room, Mrs. Wilson congratulated herself, for even at that early hour, her new mistress
was enchantingly lovely. There too, as it happened, Mrs. Wilson had heard that one of the
morning callers expected, was none other than
Lord Petersham. Well, she knew enough of that
one to hint her new mistress to a sure conquest.

Hence, armed and ready, Kitty entered the
breakfast room to find the earl and the dowager
comfortably seated and sipping their coffee.

The earl jumped to his feet, noting to himself
that his new ward had become, overnight, a veritable fashion plate. As he eyed her from head to
toe it occurred to him that this one was sure to
break hearts!

"Kitty," he said brightly as he pulled out a chair
for her. "What a charming gown." He smiled at
Minnie. "No doubt. We have you to thank for— "

He never got to finish. Kitty whipped round
even as she sat, and her blue eyes blazed. "No
doubt, *I* am not capable of choosing anything so
stylish?"

"I did not mean that . . ." the earl started to
fumble. What was wrong with him? Women never
set him at odds with himself? This was absurd. A
woman had not been produced that could make

him ill at ease, and this one, this one was nought but a child!

Minnie had been frowning as she watched her grandson. She could not recall ever seeing him so discomposed over nothing. It was most odd. "George, do be seated. And pass the salt, please." She said, taking control of a volatile situation.

"Well and as it happens, I chose this particular morning dress. Living in the country does not dull the senses, my lord. In fact, quite the opposite."

"I am very certain you are very right," said Minnie lightly. "George, the salt please."

The earl firmly planted the crystal dish in front of his grandmother and glared at Kitty. "Indeed, expands the senses, and dulls one's— "

"George, would you pass me that wondrous looking pastry. I shouldn't, but, I mean to all the same," Minnie cut in once more.

"Dulls the what? What does the country dull, my lord?"

"Tension," put in Minnie with a soft smile. "Ah, here are your eggs, my love."

Kitty controlled her little flush of temper and set herself to her breakfast. The countess chatted merrily, and it wasn't long before she had drawn both the earl and Kitty into her good humor. And it wasn't long after, that Kitty's curiosity won out and she was glancing toward the earl.

He had not joined them for dinner, and had not come home until she had long been in bed. Briefly, she had wondered if he had been with Mrs. Saltash. She put this aside and made an attempt at light conversation, describing her day with his grandmother and hoping he might, in the way of conversation, do the same.

The earl had no such intention. His head was still heavy from the effects of a convivial evening with his intimate cronies. He did however offer to his grandmother, "Ran into your dear friend, Henry Cope. He has just arrived in London from Brighton, and the sea air has not faded his delightful array of colors!" Halloway chuckled. "He is as dazzling as ever. Sent all his fondest wishes to you, my Minnie."

"Henry? What a silly fellow." She turned to Kitty. "He is better known, my dear, as the Green Man. Green is his favorite color, and it is all he wears, green satin suits."

"Faith, how odd." Kitty giggled.

"And paints his face, and it is said, eats nothing but green fruits and vegetables," added the earl shaking his head.

"No, that is impossible."

"Of course it is impossible. It's all for show and attention." agreed the earl.

"What manner of man, would want such attention? Is that the sort of men the Beau Monde admires?"

There was no time for a response as Wilson opened the door to announce, "Lord Petersham."

"Darling!" cried the countess as they turned to find a well dressed middle-aged gentleman coming towards them.

He stopped by the dowager to drop a kiss upon her cheek. "Minnie, your people told me you were in the middle of breakfast, but, I told them I would join you."

"Of course, darling. Allow me to present my grandson's ward, Miss Kitty Kingsley. Do take a seat beside her and I shall have eggs brought to you at once."

"No, no. I have already breakfasted," Petersham objected as he bent to take Kitty's delicate hand. His eyes had already clicked with appreciation to discover that the earl's ward was quite a lovely new ingenue. "Charmed, my dear." He said easily, even as Halloway called his attention. As his lordship took up his seat, he smiled to exchange a brief greeting with the earl, and set before himself on the table a lovely sky blue hand painted snuffbox.

Bless you, Wilson, Kitty said to herself. Her new dresser, had asked if she knew anything about snuffboxes, and Kitty had responded, only the little she had learned from her late guardian.

"Talk about snuffboxes with Lord Petersham, 'tis his great passion!" Mrs. Wilson had adjured her. "He will like that."

Observing the snuffbox now, this all made sense. It was certainly a very pretty thing, and Kitty was honestly able to remark, "Oh, my lord, how lovely." To herself, she noticed that the blue of the snuffbox exactly matched the blue of his superfine cutaway coat. She bit her lower lip and still could not refrain from saying so, though she told herself, it might be construed as far too forward. She need not have concerned herself. It was exactly what Petersham had been striving for, he was most delighted with her opinion, but it was her next utterance that excited him.

"My late guardian has a marvelous collection of De Louves snuffboxes." Kitty offered in the way of polite conversation. She had not expected the fevered response with which his lordship received her news.

"De Louves, you say?" Petersham's eyes were intent as he turned a direct gaze upon her, "Never say so! Why, De Louves is almost impossible to find. I have seen but two."

Kitty could not understand such intensity over snuffboxes, but was pleased to offer, "Really? Well, as it happens, I have one that Uncle Edwin gave me as a keepsake some years ago. I have it with me. Would you like to see it?"

Petersham breathed hard for a moment. Kitty had quite made his day. "Indeed! If it is not too much trouble?"

Kitty immediately rose from the table. "I will be only a moment." As she left the room, she said under her breath, "Thank you Mrs. Wilson. Who would have thought a mere snuffbox could make such a hit?"

It did a great deal more than that. Petersham was one of the Beau Monde's arbiters of fashion. As such, his opinion in all matters of ton, was highly respected. He came away from Halloway House, with nothing but praise for the dowager's new protege. Within a very short space of time, nearly everyone was anxious to meet Kitty Kingsley!

Nineteen

The dowager had gone into raptures after Petersham had left their breakfast room. "You, my dear, have made your first conquest!" Minnie had first taken Kitty into her arms and then proceeded to clap her hands together ecstatically. "Wasn't she wonderful, George?" she demanded of her grandson.

The earl had been pleasantly surprised to find Lord Petersham, who rarely bothered with an ingenue, very nearly smitten with Kitty. He had felt a sudden surge of sure pride in her, and had immediately shaken this off. What had it to do with him? Nought, so long as she did not embarrass their name. "It was brilliant of you to mention that collection of snuffboxes. Wasn't that brilliant of her, George?" The earl could see Minnie meant to go on with this, and so he conceded that it had been most unexpectantly brilliant of Kitty.

Kitty was about to take exception to his offhanded compliment, when he stalled her by putting up his hand, "Most unhandsome of me, child. Forgive me. You were superb with Petersham, and that was no little feat. Now, I must be going."

Kitty watched him leave, conscious of a sudden loss. She puzzled over this a moment. Why should she care if he came or went? Well, his presence did always seem to lend a certain vivacity. She put this aside, however, to laugh as the dowager sighed to say on and on that her success was now most assuredly insured.

Minnie continued voicing such thoughts during the course of their shopping spree the remainder of the day. Finally, Kitty put up a hand to stop her, saying with a stifled sigh, "La! For goodness sake, I only showed his lordship a snuffbox. I didn't even know very much about them."

"Yes, but, you handled yourself as though you did, and with such sangfroid, as though it was a passion you revered." Minnie sighed happily and patted Kitty's hand with affection, "Such a good girl."

In response, Kitty could only laugh this off and shake her head. They had another quiet evening, and again the earl did not show his face for dinner, but, he was there for Kitty's first roût, and then again for her first soirée, the very next evening. Both events had been a huge success.

This was due in part, as the countess believed it would be, because of Petersham's praise. He had made the ton curious about the dowager's new protégé. There too, the earl was a rogue amongst rogues. The Beau Monde lifted their brows to hear he was in charge of a young and beautiful innocent. However, the dowager's presence on the scene effectively banished any wayward notions. It was in fact, noticed that the earl's demeanor had imperceptibly altered. An air of respectability seemed to cloud his earlier, wilder days. Still, the Beau Monde watched and wondered for how long Rogue Halloway would sacrifice his hedonistic career. Nevertheless, word had it, that the earl had obviously settled in to his new role as guardian for the Kingsley chit. This had the decided effect of making all the ton curious to see just what manner of female had accomplished such a feat.

Armed with Lord Petersham's generous praise, the countess's potent popularity and her own vivaciousness, Kitty bubbled and bounced through her first introduction to the haute ton. They upon this first meeting, were in fact, certainly not disappointed. They discovered Kitty both a beauty and a refreshingly candid wit.

And then, it was Beau Brummell that sealed Kitty's pinnacle in the eyes of the ton, and won her the coveted title of Incomparable.

The Beau had attended the Levinson's soiree simply because word had it that the Earl of Halloway's ward would be there. He had been made curious by Petersham and, belabored by the earl who was a particular friend of his, to single out Miss Kingsley and thus insure her Season.

The Beau saw Kitty at once, across the room, being much admired by a bevy of young gentlemen. Slowly, he appraised her. Her gown of iridescent bronze was low cut, lower than what was usually allowed to a debutante. Ah, audacious, he thought and liked. Golden ringlets, very nearly white hung in careful disorder, threaded throughout with the same bronze ribbon. Topaz hung from Kitty's ears and a pendant of the same from her delicate neck. A tasteful beauty, not in the usual style, he thought, and just at that moment, as though feeling his bold scrutiny (which indeed, Kitty had) she looked up. Her blue eyes flickered, and then twinkled in response to his appraisal. Beau Brummell's interest, long ago bored by pretty faces, was immediately caught!

Kitty had *not*, upon discovering his audacious inspection, looked away in modest confusion. She had *not* subjected him to a missy show of whimpering and blushing, and she had not put up a haughty chin to rebuff him. The Beau was taken aback and intrigued.

Indeed, the truth of it was, Kitty had suddenly realized with great pleasure, an extremely well dressed, pleasant looking gentleman unabashedly surveying her. She was amused, she was flattered and she responded by inclining her well shaped head, giving him a saucy look, before correctly returning her attention to her surrounding throng.

The Beau sucked in air and for the first time in many years felt his heart pulsate. Purposely, he made his way across the room, totally unaware, and unconcerned that every eye, including that of the Earl of Halloway's was watching his progress.

All conversation had expectantly stopped, as the young men around Kitty discovered the Beau, whom these young men of fashion aped in the extreme, descending upon them.

"Miss Kingsley," Beau Brummell said as soon

as he had reached her side. "May I take the privilege of friendship and secure your company for a moment . . . or two?" His voice was very nearly a drawl and he spoke in a tone that depicted little interest regarding the outcome.

Kitty laughed. "But, sir, we are *not* friends, and I don't even know who you are."

A gasp from the young men around her, and then a rush of good natured chuckles. "But, Miss Kingsley, this is the Beau, Beau Brummell!" one of the young men offered.

"And my friendship is with your guardian, Miss Kingsley, and hopefully, in the near future, with you." The Beau smiled as he elegantly bent his arm toward Kitty. The assembled company seemed to be holding their breath. Never had they seen the Beau single out a debutante in such a manner. What was it about this new golden haired ingenue that had enchanted the Beau himself?

As to Beau Brummell, he was contemptuous of the society that had made him King of Fashion. He never gave them a thought, though the women on all sides fell to whispering as they watched him take Kitty aside.

Kitty gave him her gloved hand with a smile and asked softly, "You are a friend of the Earl?" She frowned as she noticed a great many people looking furtively their way, "Is something wrong?" She looked down at the narrow skirt of her gown. "Is my hem torn or . . . is something showing that should not?"

Beau Brummell laughed. "No, my dear. Your appearance is perfect."

This was said loud enough for Princess Lieven to overhear. She gasped and quickly took this as her duty to repeat to Lady Jersey only a few feet away. "Did you hear what he said to her? Faith! He told her that her appearance was perfect. The Beau has never said that to anyone before!"

"Did he? Well, I still say, her gown is far too low for a miss just out!" snapped Sally Jersey. She could see for herself that this new Kingsley chit would soon be all the rage, and her jealousy nipped at her.

"I don't think they should stare. Don't you find it most impolite?" Kitty was saying to the Beau as they strolled to a quiet corner.

He laughed again. "Most impolite, but it is the fashion."

"Absurd." Kitty laughed.

"Ah, you and I know better, don't we my dear. For in the end what does it signify?"

"Just what I have been asking myself, ever since I arrived in this mad town." Kitty's blue eyes were alive with mischief.

"Ah, but, Miss Kingsley, you were made for this mad town, don't you think?"

"I don't know about that," sighed Kitty. "Shall I tell you a secret?"

"Yes, please do."

"Before I came to London, I was wont to turn up my nose at fashion."

"Indeed?" The Beau laughed.

"Oh, yes. I was found more often than not, wearing boys' breeches and riding about the countryside unchaperoned. I was very very happy."

The Beau was again seen to laugh and without any restraint. He then eyed her speculatively. "Do you have brothers, Miss Kingsley?"

"No, sir, I do not, why do you ask?"

"Where then, did you get your breeches?"

She beamed. "We do have shops, even in the wilds of the New Forest, you know. You see, I like riding astride."

He smiled warmly. "Shall *I* tell *you* a secret?"

"Oh, yes, it is only fair, after all."

"This . . ." he touched her forehead, "and this . . ." he touched the region of his own heart, "are the things that make a soul. I trust your new and dazzling finery can not outshine your soul."

She smiled. "You are very sweet, but things do get all terribly muddled here in town, and I wonder . . ." she hesitated.

He finished for her, "You wonder just why you allowed yourself to be put on the block?"

"Exactly, sir, exactly. It is as though a woman must sell herself?" Kitty wrinkled her nose, "It is most demeaning."

He cut her off. "Do as *you* will. I don't think, Miss Kitty Kingsley that such as you, can be demeaned."

They were interrupted by the earl at that moment. He had been watching, pleased with his friend for having done him the favor of singling out Kitty with the World on the watch. This would insure her Season. He would have her married, off his hands and his fortune secured with or without Harry Brentwood! However, this sudden sure knowledge brought his dark fine brows together in a frown.

Damn, he thought as he watched the Beau thoroughly enjoying himself in Kitty's company. How the devil had she managed to enchant Brummell in such a short space of time? Watching the arbiter of fashion, he could see that there was no doubt that the Beau was definitely flirting with Kitty! How could that be? The Beau always insisted that dalliance was far too strenuous and refused to be pulled into the sport. Besides, everyone knew, he had but one love, Lady Hester. Right? Well, it was time he joined them. A moment later, Kitty was looking up to find the earl towering above them.

"My lord." Kitty greeted him with a smile. It occurred to her that the earl was the most handsome man in the room.

"Take yourself off," drawled the Beau. "We do not need you."

"I am very sure you do not." The earl smiled as he inclined his head. "However, my grandmother requires Miss Kingsley to attend her." He bent his arm to Kitty.

"A trump card, eh, George? Very well, you may play it." The Beau's bright eyes glittered appreciatively as he addressed Kitty with an elegant bow. He came up from this unobtrusively taking her fingers to whisper, "I feel moved to tell you, my dear, that I look forward to the next time we meet with great anticipation."

"So do I," said Kitty innocently, once again leaving the Beau chuckling in her wake.

She smiled up at the earl as she put her gloved

hand on the earl's bent arm. She could not help but notice that his arms were muscular beneath the black velvet cloth, and that his shoulders were amazingly broad. Kitty bubbled at him and he smiled to see the happy twinkle in her blue eyes as she said, "I like him. He has a wonderful mind. I can see why you call him friend."

"Can you?" said the earl tongue in cheek. "I have never really understood it myself."

She laughed. "Why *did* you take me away? Truth now."

"May I not tell you instead, that I wanted my beautiful ward to myself?"

Kitty felt the heat flourish through her body and burn her cheeks. He didn't mean it, she told herself. Why should she feel such pleasure at words that were so obviously false? She wagged a finger at him and retreated in severity to hide her momentary confusion. "Truth, I say!"

"Ah, truth? You do not appreciate the pretty?"

"Ha! What is its use? What good does it do, but lead a poor green country chit," she lowered her lashes adorably, "astray. Tch, tch, and that the very man who would call himself my guardian should be the one to try and turn my head with such . . . er . . . flattery. It is most besetting." She was teasing him and feeling wildly exhilarated.

The earl was very nearly transfixed by her deep blue eyes, by her naughty smile, by the movements that accompanied her words. It was no wonder she was captivating hardened sophisticates like the Beau. He chuckled and touched her chin.

"And do you not believe that I find you beautiful?"

"Do you?" Kitty looked long now into his warm hazel eyes and found dancing lights of amber.

"Indeed . . ." he found his voice coming in husky tones and stayed himself. This would not do, "I am very proud of my ward, and 'tis how I see you, whether 'tis legal or no."

Kitty felt deflated somehow. He still regarded her as a child. "You have done very well, evading the original question."

He put up his hands. "Right then, you will have the deuced awful truth. So be it. Truth, for nothing else will do for my vixen." He smiled at her. "It was time little one. 'Tis your early introduction to the ton and it will be better for you to mingle— "

She was not given time to consider this as a familiar voice from behind called, "Kitty, love!"

They turned to find Magdalen bearing down on them, and Kitty heard the earl curse under his breath, "Damn the fellow's eyes!"

Kitty glanced curiously at the earl and said softly. "Thought Alex, was one of your friends?"

"Indeed, and just the sort I wish were not yours!"

Kitty giggled and put her hand out for Alex who swept her a wide bow as he took her fingertips to his lips, "You beauty, you . . ."

The earl raised his eyes heavenward. Being a guardian was a most hideous office!

Twenty

Three weeks had gone by since that first meeting with the Beau. Since then, Kitty had met him often and a sure, easy friendship developed. In this time, she also had acquired a considerable following of admirers. This ranged between young gentlemen on the town for the first time, to experienced and older roues, including the Prince Regent himself!

The Beau Monde was much in love with the new ingenue and quite ready to pay her homage. The patronage of the Halloways was a strong ingredient, but could not have won her such power had she been a simpering miss or just another spoiled beauty. Young and old men alike were charmed by Kitty's casual manners and broad sense of humor. Her ready understanding of sport and its need in conversation quickly endeared her to gentlemen weary of forever having to do the polite with the ladies of their class.

Kitty's popularity immediately banished whatever fears she had regarding the fact that she lacked the polish that a select ladies seminary would have awarded her. Bolstered, because she found that gentlemen were not the only ones flocking to her side. She had managed in a very short space of time, to gather any number of female acquaintances eager to be in her elite corner.

However, while Kitty was enjoying her rides in Hyde Park with this new and, more often than not, witty group of young people, she knew its worth. She was excited and flattered by the ever constant barrage of posies, pretty fans, decorative posies, but she was not fooled. She looked into the souls of her newfound friends, and discovered them rather silly and shallow. Kitty's instincts took over as she scanned the bevy of young aristocratic gentlemen paying her court, and found their antics very nearly absurd. She was fairly certain that not a one was in earnest. They courted her because it was fashionable to do so, after all, she was hailed the incomparable! *Ridiculous,* she told herself. She did like flirting with the older, more sophisticated cavaliers, and never took any of their outrageous dalliance seriously. It was, simply, good fun, and she was not so green that she could be taken in by their extravagant exertions. The truth was that at bottom, she missed Harry, she missed Henrietta and she missed her home.

These thoughts mingled in her brain as she sat bolt upright and stiffly in the Halloway box at Drury Theatre. Though she seemed to be gazing at the stage and at Kean who had been wildly spluttering his lines in his role as Shylock, she really paid little heed.

The countess, who was seated beside her, seemed to be genuinely enjoying the performance. In fact, she appeared spellbound. Well,

Kitty knew herself to be the odd one out, in her opinion of the new actor. Kean was the favorite, the hailed theater great amongst the Beau Monde. Few spoke a word against him. Lord Byron, whom she had met some nights ago, told her, that Kean's acting had captivated, thrilled and terrified him. Well, she found the fellow quite a detestable little man. She could not see what all the fuss was about. There was not a terrifying thing about him.

Sighing, Kitty glanced round the galley and the other boxes, all full to capacity. Indeed, everyone seemed absorbed in the play. She made a face and wondered at it all, before taking a look in the earl's direction. He sat on the other side of her and she had been all too conscious of him most of the night. She studied his profile. Faith, he was so very handsome, so very magnetic. She had quickly learned during her time in London, that he was considered quite a marriage prize, and after weeks in his company she could not deny the fact. They were rarely at odds these days, and in fact, often found many instances where they eyes would meet across the room in mutual amusement over one thing or another. Indeed, she had learned that the earl had many redeeming qualities. However, he could be extremely arrogant, opinionated and insufferably stubborn, as well.

She smiled to herself then, for she could see from his expression that he was not finding pleasure in Kean's performance. He felt Kitty's eyes on him and turned an inquiring glance her way. "What is it, little one?" He knew of course that she was heartily bored. Covent Garden would have been much more to her liking.

"He is a disgusting fellow. And he has a terrible voice. I don't care for his interpretation of the part, do you?"

"He has a certain force, but, no, my girl. I don't care for Kean, though all the world does!"

"That is something I greatly admire in you," said Kitty thoughtfully.

He chuckled quietly. "That I don't like Kean?"

She slapped his arm playfully which caused Minnie to admonish her to quiet, so she lowered her voice. "Absurd. No, I like that you don't give a fig for the opinions of the World . . ."

"Ah," said the earl feeling a ridiculous sense of pleasure, "And here I thought you did not like a thing about me?"

"I didn't . . . at first. You infuriated me, you see, but, now . . . well, I don't dislike you quite as much."

"Shhhhh." The dowager glared, but had the dark not hidden her eyes, Kitty would have seen them twinkling.

Intermission came, bringing with it two of Kitty's young gallants. Kitty invited them to sit and tell them what they thought of Kean. Both made the fatal mistake of thinking him the greatest actor alive. Her blue eyes opened wide and she cast the earl a desperate look. Halloway laughed outloud and stood up, excusing himself as a few of the dowager's elderly friends entered their already crowded box. Kitty attempted to halt the earl from leaving her with the most dandified of all her beaux, by reaching out her hand, "My lord?"

He grinned wickedly at her. "I am going to fetch you some negus, my dear."

"Oh, no. Please, I do not wish any." She gave him a meaningful look as her gloved fingers found his sleeve.

He gently removed her hold and his hazel eyes were alive with dancing lights. "Do you not? Well, I shall fetch it to you anyway." Thus, the earl left her to her gentlemen and quickly made his escape.

Kitty was all too conscious of the earl's departure. It was as though the box were suddenly empty. What nonsense, she told herself. She was just getting too attached to his company. That was always her way. She grew used to people, used to having them about. She so disliked change.

She returned to the business at hand and abruptly diverted the subject, demanding the two dandies point out various notables presently socializing in the galley. There were many notorious aristocrats she had not yet met during her stay in London. Then all at once, she saw only one vision, one scene. She discovered the earl across he galley, in Mrs. Saltash's box. Something flickered through her senses and without realizing it, her dark lashes twitched involuntarily.

The redhead was looking particularly beautiful in a pale gold and most clinging gown. She stood, surrounded by a small group of people. Only one other woman (a dowd of a creature, Kitty correctly assumed to be a poor relation) was amongst her party. Of the men, Kitty knew only two, Alex Magdalen, and the earl.

Kitty was transfixed on this view and watched with avid interest. Here now was yet another thing she had learned whilst in London. It was reported that Mrs. Saltash meant to have the earl, and that if anyone could have him, *she* could! So Kitty watched them.

It was immediately obvious that all the party in the lovely widow's box was in high and festive spirits. Kitty could also see that it was the earl's hand the redheaded widow took to her fine cheek.

However, Kitty did not have time to observe more, for she heard her name called. The voice was so very familiar, so very dear that she spun round and nearly jumped to her feet, much startling the gentlemen at her side,

"Harry!" Kitty nearly cried as, much to the shocked chagrin of these same gentlemen, she dove into Harry's outstretched arms, "You are here. You have come!"

He gave her a hearty shake. "Yes, yes, Look at you! Egad, Kit, you are prime!"

"To the nines, Harry. To the nines! But, tell me, when did you arrive in London? How did you find me? Why have you come?"

"Ho there, zany, one at a time."

All at once the earl was there, touching Harry's shoulder to say, "Brentwood, welcome."

Harry took the earl's extended hand and gave it a firm clasp.

"How do you do, my lord."

"Harry, is everything all right at home?" Kitty started to frown with concern.

"Everything at home is fine," he started.

"Then what brings you to London, Harry?"

He blushed brightly and squeezed her hand for she still clung to his. "Not now, Kit. Suffice it to say, I *had* to come!"

The dowager was bidding farewell to her friends, and turned to Kitty. "My dear, do release the poor young man's lapel. You must not wrinkle him."

Kitty realized that while she clung to Harry's hand, her free hand held his lapel in a death grip. She laughed, "Oh, Minnie, this is Harry, my dear friend from the New Forest. He is here."

"I can see that." smiled the dowager. She turned to the other young men watching all this with keen interest and advised them, "You boys must leave now. Go on." She returned to Harry who was bending to take the dowager's lacey gloved fingers in a light touch and explain that he was a Brentwood, and very pleased to meet her.

"Of course, of course, Kitty has spoken of you a great deal. Sit!"

This done, the lights dimmed and the curtain rose. There was no time for further conversation though Kitty announced without shame, "Now, my poor Harry, you shall be subjected to Kean!"

The earl laughed outloud at Harry's doubtful expression and sat back. He had to think. Here was Harry Brentwood. No doubt, the boy had come to make an offer for Kitty? He should be pleased by this. It was what he had wanted. Yes, well, but that was before . . .

Before what, an inner voice demanded. Before it became apparent that Kitty could have anyone in all of England. Why should she settle for a country gentleman, when she could have anyone . . . a royal duke if she liked? Why, indeed?

Twenty-one

It was a clear bright April morning. May's dedication to Spring was apparent in the air, and Kitty's spirits were explosive. Harry's appearance out of nowhere at the theater the evening before, was like a soothing tonic, but there were other matters, obscure, and intangible things that had her irritated with confusion.

After the play was at an end they had been accosted by a bevy of friends and acquaintances. Even Harry had found a couple of friends he had known at Oxford. He had taken his leave in their company promising to visit Kitty in the morning. She had laughed to wave him off and turned to find the earl in close conversation with Mrs. Saltash not more than twenty feet away.

Kit had been unable to look away and then all at once, the redhead had glanced in her direction and their eyes had locked. Then just as quickly, the pretty widow's lips formed something of a sneer, before she returned her sensual glance toward the earl.

"Well, well?" Magdalen whispered in Kitty's ear. "Now what, Kitten, was that all about?"

Kitty eyed him and frowned. "Do you know, I really don't have any idea. I don't even know her."

"No, *you* don't, but, *George* does." said Magdalen, his bright eyes glittering wickedly.

"That has nought to do with me," Kitty responded her blue clicking with more emphasis than was necessary.

"She thinks it does."

"Alex, you speak in riddles, and I was never very good at them. If you are trying to make a point, do so!"

However, this was not possible as the earl had approached them by then, and Magdalen glancing at Halloway's face, laughed. "George, you madman, don't look so black! I am, but behaving the honorable gentleman, not the bold gallant. I am keeping your ward entertained while you were . . . er . . . otherwise *occupied.*"

"How convenient for you, Alex," remarked the earl dryly. "Now, however, I am *not* occupied, and you may take yourself off."

"My lord," objected Kitty with a mock gasp, for her blue eyes were alight with humor.

"Offensive fellow, isn't he, Kitten?" laughed Magdalen.

"Aha, is that wretched Magdalen bothering you, Kitty?" demanded Minnie austerely as she gave her friends a final farewell wave. "Go away, Alex, I won't have you turning my little one's head."

"But, I object, my lady. Kitty has such a pretty head," bantered Alex with a charming smile.

The dowager gave his strong arm a rap with her fan. "Never mind scamp, go find other game."

"Yes, but, Minnie, I do so enjoy having my head turned," teased Kitty archly, "for, it is not so empty that it can be *swept* away."

"Touche!" laughed the earl as he gave Kitty's chin a pinch, "Ah, our coach."

They had parted happily, though Magdalen had managed to catch her eye and throw her a kiss. She had laughed and the earl had admonished her not to encourage the devil. She had put up a shoulder and advised him saucily that she could take care of herself. He had given her a rueful look, but had not commented on this.

He had seen her and the countess to their front door where he tipped his hat and wished them both sweet dreams. Kitty had been moved to inquire, "Are you not coming in?"

"No, minx, not just yet. I am promised elsewhere."

Something inside Kitty's heart trembled and the silent question haunted her brain. Where was he going? Was it to that awful widow? The possibility disturbed her greatly. She did in fact stop the dowager at the head of the stairs to ask, "I suppose . . . the earl . . . is . . . well . . . no doubt . . . going to play cards at White's?"

Minnie eyed her for a long moment. "Curiosity, at this hour can only lead you into trouble."

Words of wisdom, though they may be, they did not help Kitty at all and sleep became impossible. Her mind was a jumble of thoughts and questions. She would dose only to awaken sharply from a

disturbing nightmare . . . and the earl was at the
heart of the worst of these!

Well, thank goodness, morning had come, and
in a very short while, Harry would call, they would
laugh together and banish all the uncertainties of
the night away. She drank the last of her morning
coffee, when a knock sounded lightly at her par-
tially opened bedroom door. Kitty called out a
welcome and smiled to find Mrs. Wilson and
Nanny briskly walking into her room. Nanny
moved to stoke the small fire in the grate. "Good
morning, my sweet girl."

Kitty met her half way and dropped a kiss on
her cheek. She was fully aware that her nanny and
Mrs. Wilson had become very nearly conspirato-
rial lately. The two had quickly developed a warm
friendship, based as it were, with Kitty's interests
as a bond. "Well, don't you two look bright and
eager today?" Kitty commented suspiciously.

Nanny smiled innocently. "Yes, and such a fine
spring day it is."

Mrs. Wilson moved toward Kitty's wardrobe,
saying almost too lightly, "And which morning
gown would you like today, Miss Kitty?"

"The ivory muslin with the red velvet trim,"
answered Nanny, who had looked in on Kitty the
night before, and learned briefly that Harry was
in town, and expected this morning. "I do so *love*
that one, and you know, dear, you haven't worn it
yet."

"No, I am saving that for next month. I shall
wear the hunter green velvet with the ivory
flounce on the half sleeves." She eyed herself in

the long looking glass. "Yes, and I shall wear my hair piled high at the top of my head!"

Nanny and Mrs. Wilson exchanged secretive smiles and knowing glances, and Mrs. Wilson offered tentatively, "Well now, Miss Diddles *did* mention that you were expecting a caller . . . a friend I take it, from home? I suppose he is a very *special* friend?"

Nanny giggled and Mrs. Wilson smiled broadly. Kitty studied both of them for a puzzled moment and then with disbelief objected, "Oooh, what silly widgeons!" She stamped her foot at Nanny and wagged a finger, "How can you be so absurd?"

The earl had breakfasted early and had already gone for a morning ride. His sleep had been a tortured series of nightmares. By six, he had ordered coffee to his room, dressed, and walked the short distance to his stables. His mind had been a collection of disordered thoughts. He stood now by the fireplace, staring into its low burning flames when he was accosted by the present.

The door of the library opened and Wilson announced in quiet tones, "Mr. Harold Brentwood."

The earl immediately collected himself and strode across the Oriental rug, hand outstretched, "Brentwood, good morning."

His warm greeting, was quite genuine, for indeed, he liked young Harry. However, inwardly he was in a turmoil, after all, he thought irritably, just what the devil was the lad doing there first thing in the morning? It was far too early for a respectable morning call. Could it be that the boy was that eager to be with Kitty again? Of course he was, dash it! He had come to seek her out at the theater, hadn't he? Timing was everything, and Brentwood's timing was damned annoying!

Halloway found himself supremely agitated by Brentwood's intrusion in a world that had become insidiously delightful and wonderfully comfortable. He had not meant to be so much a part of his grandmother's and Kitty's activities, but, somehow he had been drawn in, and had unexpectedly been finding great pleasure in the part he played.

The earl had become accustomed to this new life, to mornings filled with Kitty's enthusiasm for life. He enjoyed hearing her take on society's foibles. He had begun to like, very much, the way she would look up at his face with her deep blue eyes and confide some piece of nonsense or other. Harry's presence now would surely change all that.

"Good morning, my lord." Harry smiled warmly as he strode towards him to take the earl's extended hand. "I hope I am not too early? Kit made me promise I would be here by nine o'clock."

"And here it is, nine o'clock precisely." The earl glanced toward the mantle shelf clock.

Harry felt a moment's discomfort. There was something odd in the earl's attitude, something different.

However, Kitty arrived at that moment, resplendent in hunter green, bouncing merrily as ever, as she hurried toward her old friend. "Good morning," she said to the earl, even as she gave all her attention to Harry, taking both his hands in hers. "I can still hardly believe it. You gave me no hint in your one letter, Harry . . . *one* letter."

Harry laughed, "You know I am no good with the pen, but, at least I *did* write."

"Why didn't you tell me you were coming?"

"I didn't know then . . . It all came about rather . . . er . . . sudd . . . enly."

Kitty's dark well defined brow lifted. "I smell a mystery."

Harry blushed and glanced sideways towards the earl, "Stuff and nonsense . . ."

"You don't at all convince me, Harry. Remember, *I know you.*"

The earl was not obtuse. It was most obvious to him that Harry needed to talk privately with Kitty. The only comfort he took from this was his gut instinct which told him there was more to all this frenzy than met the eye. So be it, the earl had always believed in meeting things head on. Time would tell, and when it did, he would deal with it, whatever it might be. The Earl of Halloway inclined his handsome head and excused himself. "I do beg your pardon, Harry. I was just on my way out when you arrived. I know I leave you in good hands, and no doubt my grandmother will be down presently." He looked to Kitty and his hazel eyes softened. "My dear . . ."

Blue eyes twinkled for Kitty was not fooled, it

seemed every single day, she was discovering new depths to the Earl of Halloway, never before suspected. "You are most kind, my lord. Thank you."

The earl realized her tribute and felt his heart swell as he inclined his head, "Till later, then."

Kitty watched him go, marveling to herself. Had it been only four weeks ago when the earl had ridden onto Warton and turned her life upside down? She had thought him an arrogant, conceited blade without heart. She knew him to be otherwise now. With a soft sigh she returned her attention to Harry, as she drew him to the brown velvet sofa. "Now, sir, tell me all!"

He laughed and then with a frenzied movement ran his hand through his fair locks. "I don't know where to begin. So very much seems to have taken place after you left."

Kitty's blue eyes clicked with surprise. "Really? Just what does that mean? And do sit down, Harry."

Harry complied with her wish, but leaned forward, his elbows bent on his knees, "I don't know where to begin."

"Shall I give you a beginning? I went on my journey to London, and you were left with nought to do but click your heels . . ."

"As a matter of fact, I did miss you. Henrietta did as well." He eyed her between knit brows. "Has . . . well . . . has Henrietta not been writing? She had mentioned receiving a letter or two from you."

"She is not much better than you." Kitty returned pulling a face. "I have only received two letters from her to my *four.*"Kitty shook her head. "And one was worse than the next. A jumble of disjointed sentences. Not at all like Ree." She shook her head. "But then Ree was never much of a letter writer, either. I don't know what is so difficult about it, all you have to do is talk onto paper."

"Did . . . did she mention me?"

"Yes. She said you were well." Kitty was frowning. "Harry, just what is going on? What the deuce are you not telling me?"

"Did she mention Clay?" Harry asked, evading her question. Kitty became exasperated. "Yes, she said Clay was doing well, too. Ree was ever a tight lipped thing. I always told her a great deal more than she told me."

"Kitty, Henrietta should be arriving in London, sometime today!" Harry announced dramatically.

Kitty bounced in place and clapped her hands. "Really . . . she . . . she is really coming? For the entire Season, Harry? Oh, how wonderful."

"No. Not for the Season. Only for a few weeks to do some shopping." Harry frowned.

"Why am I beginning to feel like I am reading a gothic novel, *in chapters,* Harry?"

"Do you know who accompanies them, riding escort, so to speak?" Harry answered getting to his feet and pacing in a manner that seriously concerned Kitty. This was so unlike her steady and practical Harry.

"Who?" Kitty genuinely could not imagine.

"Clayton Bickwerth, that's who!" snapped

Harry coming to stand over her, and Kitty's eyes opened wide to see his hands form fists at his sides.

"Really?" Kitty was surprised and then suddenly a sure dawning lit. "No, I don't believe it! Never say, Ree and Bickwerth? No? Oh, I knew he was showing some interest in Ree, before I left, she told me so, but I can not believe she would be taken in by him."

Harry returned to Kitty and sat taking both her hands. "Kitty, oh Kitty, I knew you would see it as I do. You must help me."

Kitty stared at him. Here was yet another unexpected discovery.

"Oh my poor Harry. I have thought the wind blew in that direction, but Ree would only call me foolish!"

"I adore her. I think I have from the first moment we met, but I think I have lost her."

"No, don't say that. Harry. You and Ree . . . why it is my fondest wish. Yes, I shall help. The two of you would be so completely perfect!"

"Thank you, Kit, it means so much to me that you think so."

"Yes, yes, I do. And I also believe that if Clay is courting Ree, it is not from the heart. Why, he never had the least interest in her. Well, 'tis my belief that he is leading her toward a marriage of convenience. I know Ree would detest that." She shook her head. "Has Clay offered for her?"

"No, but I believe he is expected to. And Kit, I think her parents are well satisfied with the match."

"And Ree? How does Ree feel about Bickwerth?"

"I am not sure. I thought I had reason to believe, Henrietta was not indifferent to *me*. But lately she has denied me her company."

"Harry, let me understand this? Are you trying to tell me that Henrietta actually has spurned you?" Kitty was incredulous.

"Well, not exactly. But after the Ritters' ball, I came to call and she wouldn't see me."

"Perhaps she wasn't well."

"She saw Clay," Harry said dejectedly.

"How do you know that?"

"Because, he told me."

"This is all very odd. I don't trust Bickwerth one bit."

"That is just it, you see. I could live with it . . . if she didn't want me. But Bickwerth will break her heart."

"Don't you worry. No one shall break Ree's heart. I mean to take the reins now!"

"Oh Kit, Kit." He took her in his arms and held her thankfully.

Some moments before the earl had realized that he had forgotten his grandmother's jewel case. He had promised faithfully to drop off her diamonds for cleaning on his way to his club. With a click of his tongue, he turned on his heel and hurried back toward the house, and straight to the library where he had left the case resting on his desk. He pulled up short, however, as the vision of Kitty in Harry's arms presented itself. The two pulled away quickly, sharply, guiltily, the earl thought, and the entire experience served to make the earl loose his color and then regain it in force!

Twenty-two

It was with more control than he thought he possessed that the Earl of Halloway maintained when he finally spoke to say with frigid resonance, "I see my grandmother has not yet been able to join you?" The bite was in every word, and young Brentwood realized at once what the earl had assumed. He jumped to his feet and ejaculated with more haste than thought, "My lord, I do apologize . . . the fault was mine . . . not Kitty's, I should not have stayed but for the fact that Kit and I are forever alone . . . no, what I mean is—"

"Harry, there is no need for all this fuss." Kitty cut in, though she was unable to meet the earl's disapproving eye. "We have nought to explain." Her chin went up defiantly, even as her blue eyes glinted and discovered the earl's hazel eyes lit with amber, glinting in return.

The moment was saved, and the words set aside for another day, as the countess appeared then. She spied her jewel case in her grandson's hand. "Ah, thank you, George. You remembered. Do tell them I must have them back by tomorrow." By then she discovered Brentwood, who had immediately and nervously walked toward her, and her delicate grey brows both went up with genuine surprise. "You are Kitty's friend from the country. Well, listen to me young man, we do not keep country hours here . . ." Minnie was wagging a finger.

Kitty interrupted her with her laugh and went to hug her. "No, please Minnie, don't read poor Harry a lecture. He came at my bidding."

"Did he? Well then, child, don't go ordering these poor rascals to call on you so early. It isn't seemly I don't like to be sent for before ten o'clock."

"*I* didn't send for you, Minnie," returned Kitty saucily. She turned bright blue eyes toward the earl.

"No, I don't suppose you did, but I have a well trained staff, my girl," Retorted Minnie with narrowed eyes as she pinched Kitty's nose. "Well, never mind, the scamp is here, we might as well entertain him. Do pour us some tea."

Kitty was surprised. She had thought the earl had sent for his grandmother to chaperone her. She moved to the sideboard and began preparing the tea when the library door opened once more and Wilson appeared in its threshold to announce in stentorian tones, "Lord Magdalen."

"Zounds! More Kitty?" ejaculated the dowager. "Well, well, at this rate, we shall have a household by eleven!"

The earl had stayed long enough to witness two more arrivals make cakes of themselves over Kitty.

He smiled to himself and hurriedly made his excuses as he took his leave of the party.

Harry stayed only long enough to discover that Kitty had collected a great number of admirers in London. The library was full to overflowing with fashionable young men before he too made good his escape some twenty minutes later.

However, Kitty made short work of her callers, dismissing them glibly with excuses of her own. Within a few moments she had donned a spencer of cream and hunter green, which perfectly matched her gown. She set a beautiful matching silk confection on her golden curls, and pulled on her gloves. The dowager, who had already noticed that the carriage was waiting out front, cast Kitty a dubious eye and demanded, "Where, my dear, do you think you are going?"

"Oh, Minnie, I shan't be long. I know we are promised at two o'clock at Mrs. Rawlins. A friend of mine, Miss Henrietta Hawkins and her mother are putting up at the Claridge. I am going to pay her a visit."

"As you should, but, not, my girl, without your maid. Go on, pull the bellrope and request her to join you."

Kitty frowned. Being in town was so cumbersome. She missed her free, easy ways, but, she knew Minnie well enough to understand that certain things were not negotiable. She had grown very fond of the dowager, and would not for the world give her cause to fret. "Oh, very well . . ."

A few minutes later, the dowager happily waved her off. She was well pleased with Kitty. Her

grandson had led her to believe they would have
a tedious job attempting to regulate what he
thought was a hoyden of a girl. That had not
turned out to be the case. In fact, the dowager had
watched her grandson closely as of late, and in
her opinion he cared a great deal more for the
chit than he was willing to let on. Well, that was
neither here, nor there, she told herself contentedly. What mattered was she had quickly learned
to love Kitty and was happy to see how well the
child had acclimated to town. Indeed, Kitty would
do. However, it would be a pity if she ended by
marrying that young pup, Brentwood, the dowager mused as she lay back against the pillowed
settee. He certainly was an excellent fellow, a nice
young scamp, but not at all the sort Kitty needed.

Kitty found Henrietta alone and kicking up her
heels in her suite at the Claridge. Henrietta's
mother exhausted after their journey from the
New Forest, was resting quietly in her bedcham-
ber.

When Kitty was admitted by Mrs. Hawkins elderly maid, Ree jumped to her feet and went to her,
hands outstretched, "Kit, how did you know? I
was just sitting down to write you a note."

"Harry told me," Kitty said squeezing her
friend's hands, and was astounded to see her
friend blanche.

"Harry . . . are you saying that . . . Harry is in
town?" Ree seemed greatly agitated over this piece

of information. "When . . . when did he arrive in London?"

"Yes, Harry is in town. He arrived yesterday." Kitty answered, still studying her friend's face.

"Oh, well." Ree's hand fluttered as her lashes brushed her cheek, "No doubt his father sent him here on some business. Why else would he have come? I am sure he must be distressed to have torn himself away . . ." Henrietta allowed her voice to trail off, before finishing the sentence.

"Torn himself away? From what, pray?" Kitty pursued, her brows drawn together.

Henrietta waved this off, "From hounds and such . . ."

"Ree, don't be absurd. The hunting season is long over and you know that well enough!"

"Yes, yes, but now, tell me what is toward? Are you madly in love with anyone yet?"

"Silly goose! Love? Dandies and rakes! London is full of them, and *I* am not interested." Kitty laughed. "But, nevertheless, it is good fun, you know."

"Yes, I can well imagine, if you are hobnobbing with Beau Brummell and Lord Petersham." Ree smiled.

"And you, Ree, who are you hobnobbing with? I hear Clay escorted you and your mother to town?"

Henrietta blushed a deep shade of red. "Yes, he did."

"And . . ." Kitty probed.

"And what?" Henrietta made a feeble attempt to dodge.

"This won't do." Kitty wagged a finger, "Out with it, girl. What is going on?"

"Clay's attentions toward me are most marked," Ree said quietly as she lowered her eyes.

"And *your* attentions, Ree?" Kitty studied her.

"He is so very handsome . . . so very charming. What girl wouldn't find his advances . . . welcome?"

"What kind of an answer is that? You are not running for office, my friend, and I am not a voter!"

Henrietta laughed outloud and hugged Kitty to her. "Oh, Kit, 'tis so wonderful to be with you again. You always have a way of dispersing the fog, don't you?"

"What is the mystery, Ree? Come clean." Kitty was not giving up.

"The mystery is that I just don't know my own mind."

"Impossible. You always know right from wrong, good from bad." Kitty shook her head. "Are you trying to tell me, you don't know your own heart? Is that it?"

"I don't know . . . perhaps."

"Really?" Kitty did not believe her.

"Oh, enough about me. Tell me about you! Are you behaving? You look absolutely breath-taking. Your clothes, why, Kit, they are perfect for you."

"Yes, I can't imagine what they cost. The dowager just sends all the bills to the earl, though why he should cover their cost, is more than I can fathom."

Henrietta, whose father had often mentioned

Kitty's name in regards to general business affairs in the last three weeks, was about to clear up this mystery for her, when the sitting room door was opened once more to admit Clay Bickwerth.

The earl left Manton's where he had shot off a few very excellent rounds, examined a friend's new firing arm, laughed heartily with a few acquaintances, and felt the better for it. His mind was still at discord with its own logic. He wanted Kitty married off, did he not? Indeed, but, only to the right man. Thus far, he had not met the right man for her. After all, he had discovered that Kitty was an exceptional woman, a child, in many ways, but upon reflection, there wasn't a thing he would change about her!

Indeed, her smile had the power to draw on his better self. Her ideals, though very often naive, were most endearing. He would hear her giggling in another room and be drawn to the sound. He could hear these thoughts as though played back for him to study, and became disgusted with himself. Nonsense. All nonsense. However, he was determined that he would not give Kitty to any ordinary fellow.

Clay made a fuss over Kitty, marveling over her hair, her grown up style, and secretly began calculating the cost of clothes that certainly came from a modiste of the first stare!

Kitty was on the alert. If Harry's suspicions

were correct, and her instincts told her that they were, Clay Bickwerth was courting Ree only because she was an heiress. Now Kitty understood that these things were done. She understood, that Clay might have no choice but to marry a rich wife, yet Kitty believed in playing fair, in being honest . . .

"Do you join us, Kitty?" Clay interrupted her thoughts to ask.

"Join you?"

"Oh Clay, I am sorry," stuck in Henrietta immediately. "I know I did say I would take a stroll with you this morning by the Serpentine, but although Mother is resting, I expect she will be getting up shortly and I am promised to her for the day."

Clay did not look very disappointed. Kitty glanced toward Mrs. Wilson who was sitting with the Hawkins' maid by the fire and having a cosy chat. Thus, assured that she would not be overheard, she moved to take Henrietta's shoulders. "Right, but tomorrow morning, my girl you are mine. We shall go and view the Elgin Marbles!"

"Oh faith! Must we?" laughed Henrietta.

"No, that isn't where we are really going," offered Kitty in a quiet voice.

Henrietta gasped. "Kitty! You will never change." Ree hugged her then and added, "Thank goodness."

Kitty laughed and wiggled her fingers as she called. "Wilson, we had better get back if I am not to keep the dowager waiting."

"I will walk with you." offered Clay, who then

turned to bow low over Henrietta's hand. "I hope I may be allowed to call on you later in the day?"

"Of course." Henrietta smiled and waved them off.

Kitty turned to Clay outside the door and eyed him openly,

"Well, my buck, you may now tell me just *what* is going on?"

Twenty-three

The earl had been walking casually, completely preoccupied with thoughts of Kitty. He was berating himself for having become too involved in the business. His duty was to see her married. Yet, somehow . . . This was left in mid-thought when the vision of a golden-haired beauty, on the arm of an Adonis stopped him in his tracks. The fact, that these two were standing with the Claridge Hotel at their backs boostered his shock. "What in thunder!"

A moment later and with sure purpose he started across the busy avenue, but he was not in time. Clay had already handed Kitty into the Halloway coach.

Well, what the deuce was going on? He was quick to note that at least Kitty had her maid in tow. He stood frowning, watching Clay jaunt down the avenue in the opposite direction. The Claridge was an elegant, exclusive and extremely expensive hotel, well beyond Clay's means. Well, perhaps he was in London to make a good showing? Indeed, the earl wished him well, but *not* with his Kitty.

He had *not* been on his way home, but now he abruptly changed his mind and his direction. His

Kitty? A voice in his mind demanded to know when she had become his Kitty? Yes, well, he was in charge of her welfare, wasn't he? His late uncle had trusted him to see to her future, hadn't he? He shrugged off any doubt of motive and applied himself to Kitty's latest perfidy. A young miss, even escorted by her maid, could not, must not meet a gentleman at his hotel! This sort of easy behavior, as innocent as it no doubt was, could not be allowed to continue. Hackles up, he hailed a passing hackney and ordered him to Halloway House in Kensington where he meant to have a word with Kitty!

However, the dowager unwittingly thwarted the earl's plans. Having donned her bonnet and gloves, she waited only for the signal that Kitty in the coach, had pulled up to their curbing. She was outside in a flash and hurrying down the short steps motioning all the while for Kitty to stay put.

"What?" Kitty laughed. "I am a full ten minutes early!"

"So you are, which gives us just enough time to stop by and pick up that shawl I admired yesterday. Decided to have it!" said the dowager with a twinkle in her faded eyes. She was enjoying herself immensely. Kitty had been the very tonic she needed since Shawna had left with Roland.

Kitty laughed. Impulsively she gave the dowager a hug, before hurriedly bidding Mrs. Wilson, who was alighting from the carriage, a good afternoon. Kit then naughtily leaned out to merrily advise Max, that they now wished to be taken to the House of Lace.

She turned to Minnie as Max started the horses' up once more and wagged a finger. "Ten minutes will never do, you know. We are bound to be late getting to your friend."

"Never mind. It is bound to be a squeeze, we shan't be missed at first, and just as they begin to look for us . . . *voilà*, we will be there!"

Just at that particular moment in time, the earl had jumped out of the hackney and realized his coach was rounding the corner out of sight. Max wasn't turning the coach toward their stables? Where the deuce was he going? Damn . . . could Kitty be off again? Frowning he looked toward the house and immediately saw Kitty's maid entering the house alone. Bloody Hell! This was damned annoying. Where could she have gone already? He hurried up the front steps after Kitty's maid in a complete flurry of irritation.

Wilson opened the door wide and the earl immediately spied Kitty's maid just going up the central hall stairs, "Wilson," he called as he moved in her direction. "Is your mistress not here?" He didn't wait for an answer, as he hurriedly added, "And if not, can you tell me just where she has gone off to now?"

"Yes, m'lord. She and her ladyship have gone to the Rawlings' Tea . . . but, I think, first they are stopping by a shop in Bond Street to pick up something for the dowager."

"Thank you, Wilson." He said on a low note. He was frowning darkly and thought he knew the cause. Kitty could not be allowed to drag the Halloway name through scandal simply because she was too naive, or too willful to adhere to the proprieties. He was itching to confront her. He wanted to stop her if he could from ever meeting Clay anywhere, and especially never when she was alone. Had Clay perhaps, discovered that Kitty was if not actually an heiress, quite happily wealthy in her own right? Had he decided she was the best game on the table? Well, the earl was determined that neither Clay, nor, Magdalen (who was also showing signs of being in earnest), would have her. In fact, he knew of no one at that particular moment in time, that was worthy of having his Kitty!

Well, now, there was nothing for it. He would just have to wait until dinner to confront Miss Kitty Kingsley, and put an end to such outrageous behavior. An inner voice advised him that his grandmother was better equipped to handle Kitty. He should do no more than diplomatically apprise Minnie of the situation, and remain distanced from it. However, he shrugged such cowardice off, bolstering himself with the notion that even his capable, indomitable grandmother, might not be able to control Kitty's willfulness! Oddly enough, he had some time ago, delegated control of Kitty's general welfare completely to himself!

Somewhat later than they were expected, Kitty and the Countess of Halloway, made quite an elegant entrance into the Rawlings' opulent and most spectacular drawing room.

Mrs. Rawling was known for her lavish affairs. Her husband was both wealthy and loving enough to indulge her whims and extravagances. Thus, she had chosen to decorate the room with an overwhelming quantity of oversized flower arrangements. Vases of mixed floral collections, as well as hot house orchards, and potted tulips, were everywhere. A professional harpist played diligently in one corner of the room, and as Minnie had promised, it was a most crowded and buzzing affair. Notables, consisting for the most part only of the aristocracies' ladies, huddled in cliches, eyeing one another. Only a few men had been invited, among them the Beau, though he would only put in a brief appearance, as would Lord Petersham. The notorious Green Man was there in full color (bringing down the Beau's censure on his head) and of course, Mrs. Rawling's son, Rupert.

As it happened, Rupert had only just come to town. Luck would have it that he fell in somehow with Mrs. Saltash and became instantly enamored with the red headed, lovely, older woman. This was a liaison, Mrs. Rawling was anxious to pulverize. However, Mrs. Rawling was a wise mother who knew that matters of the heart (even a puppy's) heart, must be dealt with delicately. Thus, when Rupert had requested her to invite Mrs. Saltash she did not hesitate to do so. She had an ace in her hand, and that ace was Kitty!

Mrs. Rawling had met Kitty only a few nights past, but she knew that Kitty's fresh, exuberant style would interest her young son. Mrs. Rawling may have secretly hoped that Kitty and her dear Rupert might take. However, what was important, was that she was certain Kitty might prove invaluable in diverting Rupert from Mrs. Saltash. It was not only the fact that the widow was six or seven years older than her darling. It was not only that Mrs. Saltash *was* a widow, and had been notoriously carrying on indiscreet affairs for years. It was that Mrs. Rawling was sure the merry widow did not give a fig for Rupert!

Thus, no sooner did the dowager and Kitty enter the drawing room, when they found themselves besieged. The dowager was immediately and happily surrounded by a group of her intimates ready for gossip, and Kitty was carried off to meet Rupert.

Rupert was an extremely nice young man. He was just down from Oxford, just one-and-twenty, and in many ways more than a little innocent. He and Kitty fell into an easy friendship almost at once. They had horses, hounds and hunting in common. To add to this, Rupert had hunted the Quorn! This made his hunting accomplishments almost godlike to Kitty, and she pleasantly hung on his every word as he recounted his hunting experiences in that region.

His mother watched discreetly and smiled to herself. In another part of the room, and less discreetly Mrs. Saltash observed her latest flirt falling under the new chit's charm. The lovely redhead was already quite irritated by Kitty's emergence on the London scene. She was secretly lividly jeal-

ous that Kitty now held the title of incomparable
as she had held that title in years past. In addition
to this annoyance, Felicia Saltash blamed Kitty for
effectually taking all of the earl's time, and attention. This new chit was playing havoc with the
widow's designs on Halloway, and welling up a
sure resentment in the widow's hard heart. If
these things were not enough, there too, was Magdalen. Now Alex was, and never could be more,
than a skilled and artful lover. However, he had
not visited with her for some days, and word had
it, that he had marriage on the mind, and was
courting the new diamond, the Kingsley chit!

Now this, Felicia Saltash found impossible to
deal with, because Alex Magdalen, king of roues,
had never courted a woman, any woman, including herself, for anything, but bed. Bitter, resent-
ful, jealous, Mrs. Saltash certainly was not at all
pleased when she gazed now at Rupert and Kitty.

Kitty felt herself being watched. She looked
round and noted that Mrs. Rawling hurriedly
looked away, and Kitty's thoughts clicked into
place as she smiled to herself. However, something else caught her eye.

The lovely redhead, Mrs. Saltash, there across
the room, dressed to the nines, her green eyes
alight with anger, and staring in her direction.
Kitty smiled tentatively, confusion covering her
with momentary shyness. She had seen Mrs. Saltash on many occasions, but they had not yet, been
introduced. Kit was surprised when the widow
nodded, and just a bit nervous to note that the

widow was moving in her direction. She was the earl's flirt.

Kitty's attention was immediately recalled by Rupert, and Mrs. Saltash was forgotten in the merriment of the moment, as they laughed over his boyish anecdote. However, a soft, drawling voice superbly called them both to order, as Felicia Saltash, claimed her prey, "Rupert, you must introduce me to your *little* friend."

Kitty's temper flew into her eyes and no sooner had Rupert completed his introductions did Kitty smile sweetly and remarked, "Indeed, I can see why you think me young, Mrs. Saltash. I suppose everyone begins to look young, after one reaches a certain age."

Rupert nearly choked as he attempted to stifle a laugh and Felicia Saltash, past the time of blushing, raised a brow. This chit had a tongue? Well, well, "When that happens, dear, I shall let you know." She turned to Rupert, "Darling, do give me your arm. I should like you to introduce me to that woman with the turban. Your aunt, I believe."

Rupert had no choice, but he cast Kitty an apologetic glance, and said softly, "I hope we may talk again soon."

"Yes, indeed." Kitty turned and found the Beau.

He touched her elbow and winked. "I am leaving you now, but first little devil, up on your toes and kiss me. I saw the Saltash have at you, and you gave her a well deserved set-down. What a good Kitty you are, and with such neat claws. I am quite proud of you."

Kitty laughed and did as she was bid. "I was very rude, though, wasn't I?"

"Indeed, you have learned very quickly. Bravo, my child, bravo!" He started off then, but Kitty called him back hurriedly. "Wait, Beau. Tell me, how can my earl love someone like that?" Her chin moved in the widow's direction.

"Love? My dear, who said anything about love," sneered the Beau, before giving her a wink and leaving.

Now, what was that supposed to mean? Was the Beau saying that the earl did *not* love the widow? Kitty had heard that he was much attached to the widow? She had assumed he was in love with Felicia Saltash. She frowned over this, for she was not so naive as to believe a man had to be in love to have a mistress. Was she his mistress? Why did it give her a pang of unhappiness to think so? Just what was Felicia Saltash to the earl? And should it matter? The point was, it did matter, so very much and it was time, she told herself to ask herself why! Just why did it matter . . . so very very much?

Twenty-four

The dowager had planned a simple dinner for that evening. They had been gadding about for the last few weeks and she felt they all needed a break from their hectic schedule. The dowager, was glad she had planned this particular evening off, as she was especially exhausted after their afternoon at the Rawlings.

Kitty had chosen to don a simple gown of sky blue velvet, for their quiet evening, however, nothing could have set off her fair beauty more. Her large blue eyes were enhanced by the color of her gown, and glistened brightly in happy anticipation of a cozy evening. Her golden tresses, simply threaded with a narrow, matching blue velvet ribbon were set in a mass of long ringlets that cascaded upon one another from the top of her head to nearly the middle of her pretty back. She stood quietly alone before the small fire in the library and attempted to collect her thoughts, and feelings. The library door opened, and the earl, looking magnificent in a cutaway of dark blue superfine, entered.

Kitty could not help but stare as he approached. His presence was like a magnetic force. She felt drawn to him, she felt mesmerized by him, and a certainty suddenly raised its frightening truth, and took hold of her brain. All at once, she knew beyond a shadow of a doubt just what she felt. A complete understanding of her emotions focused into view. She was in love with the earl, and she had been for some time. *She loved him.* She loved the Earl of Halloway with all her being . . . and this knowledge filled her with dread. How had this happened? What would she do? He, this rake of all rakes, this man who could have anyone. How could he ever love her?

Kitty, overcome by this new dawning made an inaudible greeting and hurried away from him. To hide her confusion, she took up a poker and began to fiddle with the fire. He was beside her in a thrice, taking it from her and remarking impatiently, "You will dirty your pretty gown."

She smiled tentatively. "Oh, do you like it?"

"Yes, very much." He was finding it hard to breathe. What was wrong? His temper, no doubt? He was still irritated by this afternoon's incident. He dove right in. "Kitty, I know you are used to your freedoms, but, I thought you had come to understand, that here in London, proprieties are everything."

"For goodness sake." Kitty threw up her hands. "What in blazes have I done now?"

"That, for instance, is not how a lady speaks!" He thundered at her as he took a step closer, his mien full of brimstone, and his agitation all out of proportion with the crime.

Her exasperation turned into anger. Her finely

winged brow went up. "I thought you knew by now, my lord, I have no desire to be a lady."

He lost all ability to speak and without realizing how, or why, he had her in his grip. He was bending to taste her wondrously full cherry lips before he knew what he was about. His mouth closed on hers and he enveloped her little provocative body in his embrace.

Kitty lost herself in that kiss, in his arms. Her own arms went round him and held him tightly even as her lips parted in supplication.

What in hell was he doing? A voice pounded at his back, pulled at his shoulders. Stop . . . she is under your protection . . . she is an innocent . . . what are you doing? He brought himself up and as though using sheer physical force pulled himself away, shoving her from him as though he were touching hot coals!

It was at this auspicious moment that the dowager glided into the room. Her old faded eyes took in the scene quickly, for there was little she did not see. It was, as she thought. She had been watching Kitty watch the earl for some weeks and had wondered what would come of it. Well, youth always manages to mishandle such things. The dowager put on a brilliant smile and began chatting idly about the menu for the evening.

The earl and Kitty had already managed to put some distance between one another, but were not able to respond to the dowager's overtures. Minnie was, however, quite determined to dispel the thick tension permeating the air. Sweetly, she took up a place on the sofa and directed Kitty to sit beside her. She required the earl to provide her with a glass of madeira. She had decided that she would set a civilized tone. Emotions needed a rest. She was more disturbed than she was letting on. She had not expected that matters would take such a bad turn. It was most odd. Just when things had been rolling along so smoothly. Timing forever the key. Obviously, the timing had been wrong. It was the fault of that nice young man from the New Forest, young Brentwood. No doubt, his sudden intrusion had something to do with this sudden rift between Kitty and her grandson.

Harry Brentwood, was at that particular moment artfully attempting to catch Miss Henrietta's attention. She was seated at a round table for five in the Claridge's lavish dining room, with her mother, two of her mother's friends and Clay, at his best. A flower arrangement on Henrietta's table obscured him from her as she took part in the lively conversation taking place at her table.

Harry's antics as he attempted to catch her eye were becoming comical and drawing attention to himself. He was about to give it all up and quit his table when fate crashed the scene.

Clay touched Henrietta's shoulder during the course of an anecdote he was relating. Ree moved away and in so doing, spilled her glass of wine. The wine caught the fine cuff of her lace sleeve. "Oh, how clumsy of me," she said softly, "Do please excuse me, Mother. I will only be a few minutes. I just want to get the worst of this before it sets. I shall return in time for coffee."

Harry nearly knocked over his small corner table as he jumped up and followed her out into the vestibule to call after her, "Henrietta."

She turned surprised eyes to him. "Harry, what are you doing here?"

"I had to see you."

She softened. "You did?"

"Harry old boy! I rather thought I'd find you in London before long," said Clay coming up behind him, and then adding in a sly voice, "Heard Sarah Anne Wrigley had come into town today . . ."

"Did she?" Harry was frowning darkly at Clay, and then quickly turning to tell Henrietta, "I had no idea."

Henrietta's hazel eyes had lit up at the sight of Harry, and she had felt her heart swell. At this last piece of information, however, her lashes brushed her cheeks and she said in a quiet voice, "Ah, Miss Wrigley, of course. Well, it was so nice of you to stop by and say hello, but I must see to my gown." She left both men and hurried off to her room.

Harry rounded on Clay. "Damn your soul, I know what your game is, Clay. I have no interest in Sarah Anne."

"Ah, but you did, as we all know, not so very long ago," said Clay playfully. He needed a marriage of convenience. His prize was nearly in hand. He knew that Harry had decided to have Henrietta now, but could not allow it.

"But you are wrong, it was a long time ago and has nothing to the point now," objected Harry, "And, mark me, Clay. When I am done, Henrietta will know the truth."

"Will she, my boy? Perhaps, but by then, my game will be won, and you will be reading about my engagement to Miss Harkins in the *Chronicle*."

Harry turned white, "She has not accepted you, yet."

"She will. I am nearly certain of that. Indeed, by the end of the week."

Harry didn't wait for him to finish, but turned on his heel and left him then. He had to see Kitty at once. She was the only one who could help him. And he needed help. He was no match for Clay's deep machinations!

Kitty was blue-deviled, blue-deviled in a way she had never experienced before. She put on a smile for Minnie, and though she made appropriate sounds at appropriate moments during dinner, she spent most of her time sipping her wine.

The earl was making half hearted conversation with his grandmother, and watching Kitty out of the corner of his eye. His black mood had slowly dissipated as he watched Kitty, and he found himself more than a little amused as he observed her signal for the footman to refill her wine glass for the third time. He knew that Kitty very rarely drank more than a glass of madeira. He could hear his grandmother, and realized she was calling his attention. What was she asking? It was something about the Beau. "What, dearest?" He turned to his grandmother, "What was that?"

"Brummell and the Prince, they seem to have had a real falling out. What do you know of it, George?"

"Oh, it has been coming on for months now," he answered quietly. It was serious, and he knew if the Beau did not find a way out of his enormous debts, they and his former best friend, the Regent, would be his finish.

"Indeed, but, to call the Prince fat— "

"If Beau said he was fat," slurred Kitty who immediately took up the cudgels in his defense, "he is fat. Besides, the Regent is fatter than fat. He is 'elle grande'." So saying Kitty fell into a fit of the giggles.

The dowager eyed her suspiciously. "George, don't let her have any more wine."

"No more wine? Pity, it makes her so peacefully docile." teased the earl, who motioned for her glass to be removed with the empty plates.

Kitty did not take the bait, and decided the only dignified course of action open to her, was to ignore him, however, dignity was lost, when a loud hiccup escaped her. She slapped her hand over her mouth, and offered a muffled apology, upon which she dissolved into walloping giggles.

The dowager and the earl exchanged amused glances, after which the dowager put her napkin on the table and advised the footman they would take coffee and dessert in the library. The earl was there to give her his hand as she rose from the table before he moved to Kitty's chair. Kitty looked up at him and all at once her fine blue eyes lost their glitter. "Yes, of course," she said quietly, "to the library. Where, I am sure you needn't do the polite and bear us company, my lord. I am very sure you must have other plans."

He stiffened. He had in fact, made plans for the evening with a group of his sporting friends, but had not meant to join them until much later. At Kitty's cool words and curt tone, he changed his mind, and inclined his handsome head in a cavalier fashion. "Indeed, as you say, I have other plans for the evening."

Minnie had watched their exchange and her eyelashes fluttered. She decided to play her own, wiser game. "Indeed, George, Kitty is quite right. You needn't mind us. Go and enjoy yourself."

"Thank you, love." He looked toward Kitty. "I shall do just that."

Kitty turned a cold shoulder upon him and would not have looked back as they had entered the central hall where the earl called for his cloak and hat.

Wilson was just opening the front door wide to admit Harry Brentwood who startled the assembled company by declaring, "Kitty!" in a most uncharacteristic melodramatic tone, whereby, he followed this up by pronouncing, "You *are* here."

"What the deuce?" Kitty ejaculated.

"Though I agree that this young man's presence, here at this hour, unexpected, is most surprising, Kitty darling, you must not go about saying things like that, you know," said the dowager amiably. "Hallo, young man. What a very odd time for you to be calling."

"So it is, and I do beg your pardon," offered Harry apologetically, "but, I . . . I need to speak with Kitty."

"Can it not wait till morning?" The earl stuck in irritably. He was frowning darkly, and his thoughts were bouncing off one another in a series of questions and unclear answers.

Kitty stared from the dowager to the earl and with her hand up, immediately put a stop to this. She would not have her dearest friend on earth treated to unfeeling town manners. It was obvious to anyone with any sensibility that Harry had been overset, "I do beg your pardon, my lord, but you must understand that Harry would not have come at such an hour, had it not been extremely important." She put up an imperious eye for she would not be brooked in this. She took Harry's arm and started toward the study, saying over her shoulder, "I shall not be long and will join you in the library, Minnie." She turned to the earl. "I do wish you an enjoyable evening, my lord. Good night."

"She's a brat, indeed, and we have been summarily dismissed, George. Ha! See me in a few moments will you, my girl? Indeed, you shall, in a very *few* minutes." The dowager's brow was up, but it was evident she was more than a little entertained by Kitty's high-handedness. "Ha!" she spat again as she turned away, "High flying manners, my dear, but, go on then, talk to your young man."

The earl had already taken up his top hat and

many tiered coat, but he stopped at that and looked round. Kitty's young man? Well, his grandmother was taking a great deal for granted. Harry Brentwood was not Kitty's *young man!* Not if he had anything to say about it.

Indeed, Kitty was about to set the record straight on the matter and clearly explain that Harry was *not* her young man, when she saw the earl spin round and glare. Well, how dare he? Kissing her one moment, shoving her away the next, and *now*, behaving as though he were her lord and master! It was all she could do to bite her bottom lip and keep still.

The earl restrained his temper, though he dearly wished to throw young Brentwood out of the house. Instead, he slapped his hat on his head, shrugged on his coat, took up a walking stick and bade them all a curt good night.

For a moment, Kitty stared after him. Vaguely, she was aware of the dowager still wagging a finger and telling her not to be long. Vaguely, she was aware of Harry tugging at her sleeve, and whispering her name, demanding her full attention. Yet, all she knew was that something of her had left with the earl. The sensation was almost overwhelming. All her vivacity was gone. Nothing. She was left with a feeling of emptiness. The earl was gone. Where? To that Saltash woman? Oh faith, how the notion hurt!

"Kitty, are you listening?" Harry was frowning.

"Yes, yes of course, Harry. Come, I think there is still a small fire in the study."

Twenty-five

"Od's life, Harry. Do stop pacing and sit here and tell me what has you all to pieces?" Kitty sighed as she took up a chair near the fire.

"It's Clay, he has Henrietta thinking I'm chasing after Sarah Anne."

Kitty's eyebrows went up. "Sarah Anne? Thought you had done with her. You told me she was a silly, and fickle piece of fluff."

"So she is, and yes, I had done with her. But, a few weeks ago, at that blasted ball you were lucky enough to miss, she had a bit of a problem with her dress. I was on hand and she asked me to help her. Kitty, we were funning, there was nothing in it, I swear. However, Clay with Henrietta on his arm, walked in just at that blasted moment—"

Kitty cut him off. "What blasted moment, if you please?"

Harry who had not sat down yet, began shuffling his feet, "Oh for the love of— it was nothing. You know what Sarah Anne is."

"I know what she is, tell me what she did?"

"Well, she was thanking me. There was no harm, it wasn't a passionate kiss, after all."

"Why Harold, you shock me!" Kitty was somewhat taken aback. "You are a horrid flirt and Ree would be right never to look at you again."

"Oh Kit, don't say that." Harry ran a frantic hand through his fair locks.

"Well, never mind." Kitty shook her head. "Did you at least go to Ree and explain?"

"She would have none of me the rest of the evening. So, there was nothing for it, I let it go till morning. I was on my way to call on Henrietta when, luck should have it, who should I run into, but Sarah Anne."

"Upon my young soul." Kitty was beginning to find this all absurd. "And who should come round the bend?"

"Precisely. Clay seems to have a nose for it, damn, if he doesn't!" Harry was frowning. "I had managed to get Henrietta aside tonight and what must Clay do but, barge in on us to insinuate that I followed Sarah Anne here."

"Is Sarah Anne here?" Kitty was surprised, but even as Harry sourly said that he only knew what Clay had told them, her china blue eyes clicked with sure dawning. "Ha! Did it ever occur to you that Sarah Anne has decided to have you after all, and that she and Clay have hatched a plot to separate you from Henrietta?"

Harry seemed thunderstruck. "No . . . why . . . how?"

"Timing, you know, is everything, and timing in this case, is too coincidental to be anything but planned," mused Kitty.

"Well, it's my opinion that truth should and

must win out. Listen to me, Harry, for this is what
we are going to do . . ."

The Earl of Halloway had decided to walk the
considerable distance to his friend's bachelor
lodgings, where he was to play cards that evening.

His mind was full with the feel of Kitty in his
arms, with the taste of her sweet mouth, with the
brightness of her deep blue eyes . . . such eyes!
Damnation! Thunder and turf! This had to stop.

What was happening to him? He had never felt
such uncontrollable desire for a young and innocent girl before. This was mad. She was beautiful,
yes, but, he had been chased by some of the most
notoriously beautiful women in London. Ah, said
his heart, there was so much more to Kitty. Such
sweetness of nature, made irresistible by a tart
quality, a sharpness ever on the alert for release.
She was wild to a fault. She was headstrong, and
she was tantalizing, but, she was, above all other
things, quite totally innocent. He was a devil. No
better than Magdalen who ruined virgins without
batting an eye. How could he have taken such advantage of Kitty? And what the bloody hell, did
young Harry want with his Kitty at such an hour?
He couldn't possibly be proposing to her, could
he? The earl stopped dead in his tracks as though
reasoning out loud with another person. No, no,
that made no sense. He took a few more steps,
slowly contemplating the notion. He started shaking his head, as he thought this out. Harry
wouldn't propose to Kitty at this hour? Why, what

would be the rush? Did he think someone else had managed to oust him in Kitty's heart? Was that it? Could that be? Would Harry propose marriage to Kitty without first applying to him for her hand? The earl frowned over this, and a voice spoke quietly in the earl's mind.

It was possible that Harry might believe you have no legal rights over Kitty.

Well damn the boy's soul, legality was nought! What of honor? The boy was honor-bound to apply respectfully for her hand.

The voice answered this harshly, it was possible Kitty's late guardian may have already countenanced the match?

Still, the earl could not believe that Harry had come for that reason this evening. Instincts, experience, gut-feeling assured him of that. What then? Just what was going on? Indeed, and why, for pity's sake, should it matter to him? She would marry Harry and then he could have his rightful inheritance and be done with escorting Kitty and his grandmother about town.

That's right . . . that was what he wanted, wasn't it? Wasn't it . . . ?

Morning came in a splash of sunshine and Kitty was up and calling for a cup of coffee at dawn! She had spent an awful night chasing off ghouls, demons and Mrs. Saltash.

Well, that was done, and she was supremely happy to be awake. Kitty was the eternal optimist. What had not seemed possible the evening before had now become a thing she could most certainly attain. She knew beyond a margin of doubt that she loved the Earl of Halloway. He was a rogue, he was a playboy used to having any woman he wanted, but, she loved him with all her being, and she was sure that if she applied herself, she could somehow make him fall in love with her in return. She only knew she must, for she was equally sure that if he did not end in loving her, she would wither away.

Now, however, she had to get out of the house, and she had to do this early, before anyone else was up and about to stop her. The dowager would insist she take along her maid, and today she needed freedom of movement! Today, Harry's happiness was at stake.

Right then, she must look her part! She set her pretty hunter green velvet top hat on her yellow curls and fixed its wide white gauze banding and angled the bow into shape. She eyed herself in the looking glass, and then put her pearl cluster earrings in place on her well shaped ears. She then twirled the short wispy curls over the curves of her ears. Her ensemble of hunter green fit her body snugly, and she was well pleased with the white and green braided frogging, which was in the height of fashion, that fastened and trimmed the skirted velvet jacket.

Good, she thought as she gave herself a final once over. I look the part. Ree will never suspect that I am taking her out for more than a stroll along the Serpentine. Indeed, behold, she giggled softly, I no longer look like the rough and tumble hoyden of Warton Castle.

Now, to begin! She snatched up her purse and hurried down the stairs. She looked round, and then rushed across the hall and out the front door. No one had been about to question her, and with a sensation of pure and mischievous excitement, she was racing down the front steps and gliding along the avenue until she finally found and hailed a passing hackney.

The earl, fully dressed in his riding clothes was at the top of the stairs just as Kitty closed the front door behind her. He frowned to himself and wondered if that was Kitty he had seen. Damnation man, of course it was, he answered himself irritably. A moment later he was sending for Kitty's maid and taking a stand, hands clasped at his back, as he awaited Mrs. Wilson in the library.

Mrs. Wilson was a woman of experience. She was not easily shaken, and was not overly concerned when the footman had come with the intelligence that the earl required her presence below.

"My lord," said Mrs. Wilson as she stood just inside the library, its door still open at her back.

"Ah, Wilson," smiled the earl attempting to put her at her ease. "I was hoping to catch an early ride with your mistress. However, she has already left the house, and I take it, without anyone in attendance."

"Yes, my lord."

"Do you know where she went off to?" His hazel eyes were lit with green fire.

Mrs. Wilson's exterior and interior calm was a trifle shaken by the intensity of the earl's gaze. "No, my lord, Miss Kitty dismissed me after I had dressed her curls."

"How was she dressed?"

"My lord?"

"Was she dressed for riding?" The earl maintained a bland tone.

"Oh, I see. No, my lord. She wore one of her favorite ensembles, the hunter green with the frogging. Perhaps she went for a walk."

"Thank you, Wilson." The earl watched her leave, and his eyes narrowed. It was certainly too early to be walking about in Hyde Park. What if Kitty had planned a clandestine assignation?

That was it. All of his feelings rushed together in a blast of sheer emotion. The thought of Kitty in a clandestine meeting with another man made him distracted and banished all logic. He had spent another restless night. His dreams had been filled with Kitty, with the memory of her lips, her touch, with the anticipation of their next encounter. He knew that he was in a trap of desire, but until this moment, he had not realized, it was love . . .

Love? Blister Love! What had he to do with such a disturbing, inhibiting emotion? Nought. He would ignore it and it would go away. That was what he must do. Right, ignore it, ignore Kitty and all her wiles. Ignore love's trappings. Right, that was the thing to do! However, instead he promptly stomped into the hall calling for his horse to be brought round from the stables, while he went in search of his crop, his riding gloves and top hat. He was going to find his little vixen, and . . . and then . . . thunder and turf! First things first. He would find her, and later he would decide what to do with Miss Kitty Kingsley!

Harry had taken a small corner table in the coffee shop. He was attempting to remain calm, but, how could he in the face of what was now so obvious?

Harry read Sarah Anne's quickly scribbled note and sneered. What a sapient little monkey Kit was. She had been so very on the mark. He was certainly no Bartholomew baby, but, he had not seen what had been staring at him. He felt a nodcock. Kitty was just a babe, and she had realized immediately. Now, of course, it was all so clear. Why had he been so blind? How could he have been so utterly stupid?

He gulped down the remainder of his strong coffee and motioned for the waiter to bring him another. Timing, Kitty had said, was everything, and he had still a few minutes before he was due to make his move . . .

"Kitty, you are early," declared Henrietta as she spun round from the vanity table to greet her friend. They had made definite plans, but she was certain the hour they set was much later.

"So I am," allowed Kitty with a negligent wave of her hand. "It is such a beautiful morning, I just couldn't wait." Kitty moved to Ree's wardrobe and pulled out a pretty straw bonnet with blue trim. "Here." She then pulled out a lovely cloak of sky blue, trimmed with straw colored lace round the hood, "and this. I love this. Put them on and let's hurry."

"Why?"

"Before your mother awakes and makes us take your maid," Kitty whispered.

"But, Kit, shouldn't we *take* my maid? I mean, we should not walk about London unattended. It isn't done."

"Yes, it is. I do it all the time and have not yet encountered any censure. After all, what is the harm. It is so early," coaxed Kitty sweetly. It was only a very small fib. She had gone off to the lending bookstore on one occasion alone, and on another, to the stables just to look in on her horse. Both times had ended with the dowager ringing a peel over her head. Yes, but it had been well worth the feeling of freedom she had felt, and this time it would be too, she was sure.

"Very well," agreed Henrietta smiling as she slipped the velvet cloak over her shoulders and clasped it at the neck.

"Perfect, that color suits you, Ree," mused Kitty as she hurried her friend out the door.

"Kitty, whatever is the rush? Allow me to pin my bonnet in place, there . . . and pull on my gloves."

"I just want to get away before we are found!"

laughed Kitty who was on a tight schedule. She glanced toward a small ornamental china clock on the side table and noted that she was in fact running much on time! Good, now if all goes just as we planned and everyone does what they are supposed to do, all will be right and tight!

Clay consulted his pocket watch. It was a family heirloom he did not mean to part with, and would not have to do so, now that he was about to contract an advantageous marriage. Indeed, he would have a dutiful, if not beautiful wife to bear him heirs and her fortune to bear him pleasure. He had nought to do, but marry her. A minor sacrifice. He would take her to the seaside for a short honeymoon, no more than a week. Yes, a week was all he could stand to think of in Henrietta's placid company. Never mind, he bolstered himself, he might be able to reduce that to five days, tell her they had to get back to the New Forest and start the exciting business of refurbishing his ancestral home! That was the ticket! He could then leave Henrietta there, and attend to other matters, his more pressing needs in London.

It was, after all, the accepted mode of life amongst his own class. Love had little to do with marriage. He would not even forbid her a discreet romantic alliance now and then.

In the meantime, however, there was an affair that called for his immediate attention. This was certainly something he could not neglect. It did have him puzzled. Whatever could be the trouble?

However, women were such jittery creatures. There was never any telling what might set them to fretting. It was very probably nought, but no sense taking any chances? Best to attend the summons he had received earlier. He shook his head over it, for he had thought everything was going along perfectly, and so smoothly? At least it was early enough that no one would really be around to observe them . . .

The earl sat his horse well as he wielded him through the hectic morning traffic. Hawkers moved about, calling out the nature of their wares for sale. One waved a loaf of freshly baked bread about and started the earl's young grey. However, the earl was ready for it and managed him easily as he headed determinedly for Hyde Park.

His eyes scanned the wide curbing, watching for Kitty, as he kept pace with the slow traffic. He saw instead, Clay Bickwerth crossing the avenue toward Hyde Park!

Clay again! He had not yet confronted Kitty about her last meeting with Clay outside the Claridge Hotel. Now here he was again, no doubt, on his way to meet Kitty. Well, this made more sense than the notion of her meeting young Harry clandestinely at this hour. So, that was why Harry found it necessary to rush in on them in a frenzy last evening? Was he jealous over Clay? Had he come to confront her? Damnation! Blister the muckworm's soul! He would have Clay's blood for this!

* * *

Harry took up an inconspicuous place behind a large evergreen along the walkway of the Serpentine. Not far away he had pinned a yellow ribbon on another evergreen. He could see Sarah Anne, with her maid at a conspicuous distance, behind her. She spotted the ribbon immediately and asked her maid to wait, before approaching the marked tree. Right on time, he could see Clay wave and hurry toward Sarah Anne, and he could just barely hear Clay say, "Sarah Anne, sweet child, how lovely you look."

Even in the midst of all this, Harry had to smile to himself, Clay was always the charmer.

Thus, with the stage set and ready, Harry hurried out of sight.

Kitty nearly dragged Ree along, as she hurried toward the marked tree. If she could just get Ree into position, and keep her quiet.

"What are you doing? Why are we cutting across the lawn? Kit Kingsley, what are you up to?" Henrietta demanded.

"You will trust me and be very still. Please darling Ree, trust me. There is something you need to see, something you need to hear." Gently Kitty positioned Ree behind a row of evergreen ornamental hedges. A little more roughly, she made her bend her head low.

"Why, that is Clay," said Henrietta on a hushed

note as her hazel eyes took in the scene with some surprise. "And Sarah Anne— "

"Shhh."

"How is Henrietta? Has she accepted to marry you? When shall you post the banns? Soon, I hope," sighed Sarah Anne. "Then Harry will turn to me in a fit of the dismals, and I shall console him . . ."

"I haven't proposed yet, I mean to do that tonight." Clay was frowning. "Is that why you sent for me?"

"Sent for you? I didn't, you sent for me. I thought you would have good news."

Clay looked around at that moment and suspicion filtered into his cunning brain. "No. I didn't send for you. I received a note telling me to meet you by the yellow ribbon along the far side of the Serpentine."

"Well, I didn't write any such thing!" Sarah Anne declared indignantly.

"Did you not? It doesn't signify. Go home, Sarah Anne. Quickly." Clay commanded as once again his eyes scanned the lawns and pathways. "Perhaps we are too quick for them." He moved toward the wide expanse of green lawn and away from her. He looked back and was satisfied to see she was already scurrying away.

"Did you hear them, Ree?" Kitty turned Henrietta toward herself to ask her again, "I said, did you hear them?"

Henrietta had pulled herself up and wasn't sure

what she was feeling as she gave Kitty her full attention. She felt foolish and that made her tone angry. "Yes. I heard them." She shook her head. "Why did you do this? Why this elaborate set up. You did set it all up, didn't you, Kit?"

"Yes. I sent them each a note. I thought I knew what they were at, but I had no proof. So, I did this. It was the only way I could show you, because you would not have believed me had I come and told you my suspicions. You would have thought I was merely trying to help Harry to prove he loves you. And he does, Ree." Kitty concentrated her sharp gaze on Henrietta's face, "What I thought you needed, was to see for yourself— "

In those moments they had been too absorbed in one another's feelings to notice that Clay had discovered them. They jumped to hear him say coldly, "How very clever all of this is, Kitty. Did you think of all this on your own?" He shook his head. "And once I thought we were close, you and I? What Kitty? Did you feel scorned when I switched from you to Henrietta? Is that it, Kitty?" He looked at Henrietta, and said in tones that sounded astonishingly sincere, "Dearest, you see, things are rarely what they seem— "

However, Ree would not be taken in with a lie once more. "Of course, they are not, Clay," retorted Henrietta caustically, "As you have so perfectly demonstrated!"

Clay lost his temper and took a menacing step toward Kitty.

"Do you know what you have done, she-devil?"

"I do," said Kitty quietly. "But we both know

you will come about. How could you not? There are other heiresses out there, Clay and any of them would be far more suited to your schemes than my Ree— "

"Really, and do you mean to point them out to me?" growled Clay as he grabbed Kitty's arm suddenly and started shaking her.

"Unhand her, cur!" Henrietta shouted much outraged at this scene.

Harry came running across the lawns and jumped the last length to land Clay a facer! Clay, who still had a firm grip round Kitty's arm, ended by tearing the sleeve nearly off her jacket as he reeled backwards, tripped and ended in the dirt bed of an evergreen.

Harry turned and found Henrietta in his arms and saying his name over and over. He kissed her forehead and immediately turned to Kitty who was a bit shaken and mumbling something about her bracelet. Henrietta spied it in the grass and hurried to retrieve it as Harry put a comforting arm about Kitty's dainty shoulders.

The earl arrived only in time to witness Harry taking Kitty into the fold of his arm. He saw Clay just getting to his feet and correctly assumed that Harry had planted him. So, Kitty had come to meet Clay, and Harry had intercepted. A fury tickled his brain and obscured all clear thinking. He charged his horse across the sweeping turf, to bring up the young hunter on the scene. He jumped from the grey, took up his reins and handed them to Henrietta, who stood before him eyes open wide. Then, and without a word, he reached to pluck Harry away from Kitty, "I have seen enough!" declared the earl in a wild rage. There was no time for anyone to respond to this, as he then immediately scooped Kitty cradle-like into his arms, and threw her onto his saddle. He then noticed Harry had his arm around Henrietta. He frowned over this, but said only as he took the reins from her, "Miss Harkins." He gave Harry a disparaging glance. "No doubt, there is an explanation for all of this, and I mean to get one firsthand." Thus, dismissing them, he took up his stirrup and swung himself up and behind Kitty, and urged his horse forward.

Kitty had been struck speechless by his appearance on the scene. It occurred to her that he was behaving much like a jealous lover and she smiled to herself, pleased with the notion. She then found herself ensconced in his arms as he took up the reins, and softly she whispered, "Just like a knight in a storybook— "

"Make no mistake, I am no knight," he said, his face still flushed with anger.

"Then, just what are you doing here, my lord?" She smiled up at him and he found himself softening in spite of his resolve.

"Looking for you, which leads us to the all important question, what are you doing here, minx? Truth now, if you please."

"I was helping Henrietta and Harry, you see, they are in love and— "

"*They* are in love . . . with *each other?*" The earl ejaculated in disbelief.

"Yes. And Clay, who needs to make a marriage

of convenience, decided he would trick them apart, and then have Ree and her fortune for himself."

"Henrietta and Clay?" again the earl was struck dumb.

"Yes, and so . . ." She looked round and up into his hazel eyes. "It is a long story that I think might end very well." She then pursed her lips invitingly and closed her eyes.

The earl laughed, and it was a joyous sound, before he was bending to kiss her lips. "Very well, my future little hoyden bride. Very well, indeed."

ZEBRA REGENCIES
ARE
THE TALK OF THE TON!

A REFORMED RAKE (4499, $3.99)
by Jeanne Savery

After governess Harriet Cole helped her young charge flee to France — and the designs of a despicable suitor, more trouble soon arrived in the person of a London rake. Sir Frederick Carrington insisted on providing safe escort back to England. Harriet deemed Carrington more dangerous than any band of brigands, but secretly relished matching wits with him. But after being taken in his arms for a tender kiss, she found herself wondering — *could* a lady find love with an irresistible rogue?

A SCANDALOUS PROPOSAL (4504, $4.99)
by Teresa DesJardien

After only two weeks into the London season, Lady Pamela Premington has already received her first offer of marriage. If only it hadn't come from the *ton's* most notorious rake, Lord Marchmont. Pamela had already set her sights on the distinguished Lieutenant Penford, who had the heroism and honor that made him the ideal match. Now she had to keep from falling ⌐der the spell of the seductive Lord so she could pursue the man ⌐e worthy of her love. Or was he?

⌐ DY'S CHAMPION (4535, $3.99)
⌐y Janice Bennett

Miss Daphne, art mistress of the Selwood Academy for Young Ladies, greeted the notion of ghosts haunting the academy with skepticism. However, to avoid rumors frightening off students, she found herself turning to Mr. Adrian Carstairs, sent by her uncle to be her "protector" against the "ghosts." Although, Daphne would accept no interference in her life, she *would* accept aid in exposing any spectral spirits. What she never expected was for Adrian to expose the secret wishes of her hidden heart . . .

CHARITY'S GAMBIT (4537, $3.99)
by Marcy Stewart

Charity Abercrombie reluctantly embarks on a London season in hopes of making a suitable match. However she cannot forget the mysterious Dominic Castille — and the kiss they shared — when he fell from a tree as she strolled through the woods. Charity does not know that the dark and dashing captain harbors a dangerous secret that will ensnare them both in its web — leaving Charity to risk certain ruin and losing the man she so passionately loves . . .

Available wherever paperbacks are sold, or order direct from the Publisher. Send cover price plus 50¢ per copy for mailing and handling to Penguin USA, P.O. Box 999, c/o Dept. 17109, Bergenfield, NJ 07621. Residents of New York and Tennessee must include sales tax. DO NOT SEND CASH.